"YOU HATE ME YET YOU WANT ME."

Laura's voice was low and drowsy. "Isn't that right Eddie?"

Eddie tore his eyes from the smooth-shaped legs, the warm inviting flesh and fought the impulse to grab her. He dug his hands into the sand, and his eyes caught the flash of a key. He picked it up. It was the key he'd given Al. The key to the safe deposit box—the key to the hundred grand.

"Where did you get this Laura?"

"I found it in Al's pocket. It's a vault key isn't it Eddie?"

Eddie glared at her.

"It must be a lot of money, huh?"

"Shut up. Just put that key back before Al gets here." He watched her lift the edge of her suit and place the key between her breasts.

Her eyes caught the yearning look in his. Her lips smiled up at him. "I was made for pleasure. That's what Al always says. What do you think?"

She let her eyes wander slowly down his body. Suddenly Eddie pulled her to him and kissed her hard on the lips. They were hot and wet and yielding. Her hands held him fiercely. A flame began in the pit of his stomach and tore downward.

"You're no good," he said. "You'd make a guy do anything. Even with his best friend's girl."

MURDER MONEY

by Jay Bennett

WILDSIDE PRESS

For
Dad and Mother
Sally, Steve, Randy

We never know when we stand at the hairline of death. We never know when our lives suddenly veer and begin to move slowly, inexorably down a road of fear, of blood, of death.

We never know.

Eddie Doran didn't know it either.

He walked down the dingy stairs of the gymnasium and out into the wintry street. The day was slowly dying into night. He hunched his big shoulders and looked bitterly ahead of him.

So it's all over, he said to himself. The whole damn thing is over and done with. I'm through. Washed up.

He clenched his big hands and stared at the passing cars, his eyes seeing nothing but a blur. The words of Al Walker, his manager, came back to him with an insistent force.

"No more fights, Eddie. Nobody'll buy you anymore. You're thirty-five, kid. An old man. It's the end of the road. It had to come; you know it. It had to."

"Yeah," Eddie muttered.

Then he sighed gently, turned and began walking down the darkening street, his huge body bent forward a bit, the gray eyes cold and tormented. And as he walked, the bitterness grew within him.

It's not right, he said to himself. I should get a chance to make a few bucks. I'm fighting almost twenty years and I come up with nothing. I got all of eight hundred bucks standing between me and the bread line. Eight hundred lousy bucks.

"Paper, Eddie?"

Eddie stopped and turned sharply. He looked down grimly at the newsstand dealer.

"What?"

"Asked if you wanted a paper, Eddie. That's all."

5

Eddie's rugged face softened a bit; a flicker of a smile passed over the gray eyes.

"Okay, Phil."

"Anything wrong, Eddie?"

Eddie took the paper from him and tucked it under his arm. The street lights suddenly went on, making the coin in Eddie's hand glisten. He dropped it into the tin tray and watched it spin and die flat.

"Nothing's wrong," he said.

"You'll turn lucky yet."

"Yeah."

"Just keep your spirits up, lad."

"They're up. Touching a cloud."

"So long, Eddie."

"So long, Phil."

And as he turned away and began walking again, he wondered how the blind newsdealer always knew him as he passed by.

Maybe it's my stumblebum walk.

Eddie's face became grim and bitter again. The full, smiling mouth was now thin and tight. The wind started up, biting into him. Eddie turned up the collar of his overcoat and began to walk faster.

When he came to Thirty-eighth Street and Eighth Avenue, he stopped, bewildered. The thought had suddenly struck him that he was walking aimlessly. He had nothing but an empty night ahead.

He stood there in the passing crowd, a lone, huge figure. The wind beat against him, blowing through his thick brown hair. His reddening face was cold and bleak.

Nowhere to go. Like I lost the world. Like I don't belong anywhere. I knew this was coming and yet deep inside of me I didn't know. That's why it's hitting me so hard now. Just taking the guts out of me.

I don't belong anywhere. Wherever I go, they'll know I'm washed up. Even if they don't, something in me will tell it to them. And that's even worse.

I'm starting to rock. Just like somebody hit me hard and the legs start to give. And then the rest of you goes. Christ, how I know that feeling. It happened to me the last two times out. I saw the punch coming and I just stood there and took it. Couldn't even get out of the way.

And I've got to get out of the way now. Or I'll go down.

"How's tricks, Eddie?"

Eddie turned and saw Farrell, the traffic cop, coming over to him. He shrugged his shoulders and said nothing.

"Not so good?"

"Not so good."

"Any fights coming up?"

Eddie slowly shook his head. "No more, Farrell," he said.

"Oh."

"Looks like the Commission put the lid on. Al can't sell me any more."

Farrell reached up and patted Eddie's shoulder. "It's for the best, Eddie."

"Yeah. I guess it is."

"Has to come to an end sometime."

"Everything comes to an end."

The street lights gleamed on Farrell's face and badge. About them was the harsh, unfeeling sound of the traffic.

"You always were a good, likable guy, Eddie. Keep that big smile going, huh?"

"I finish with nothing, Farrell."

The policeman's eyes widened with surprise. "You should have a good egg by now. You've been main go at the Garden lots of times."

"I haven't fought in the Garden in two years."

"Still you should have a nice bank account. You were never one of the wild ones."

"It's gone. How do I know what happened to it?"

"I'm sorry to hear that, Eddie."

"I helped out some guys. Threw away the rest. Who knows where it went? But it went."

As he walked away from Farrell, he began to wonder, where did the money go?

Then he started to tick off in his mind the people he had helped. They were all pros like himself. One had gone blind and Eddie had given him three grand. Then there was Tommy Avenie, two grand. Martie Price, a grand. Joe Alcan, who had been killed in the ring, four grand.

Joe had left a wife and two kids. They didn't have a dime to their names. But what the hell.

And now what have I got? And who's giving out to help

me? I don't know a goddam thing to do. I never learned a trade. I never learned nothing.

Three years high school and some books. And that's me. Christ, I've got to hole up somewhere.

Yeah, I threw away money, too. I hit the races and the girls. I was no different than the rest. But I'd like to have some of the money I gave away.

Ah, what the hell's happening to me? I gave it. I had it and I gave it. And that's that.

He stopped and passed his hand wearily over his face. His coat flapped open in the cutting wind. He hesitated a moment, then decided to go home to his rooms. He felt too tired and despondent to roam the streets. It would be better to get home. By taxi. Might as well live it up till the end.

Eddie walked over to the curb and stood waiting for an empty cab to come by. The longer it took, the more his weariness and bitterness grew. The cold was beginning to work into his bones. He was about to give up and begin tramping the long, dreary blocks crosstown, when he saw the dome light of an empty cab.

"Cabbie!" Eddie yelled, waving his hand.

The yellow car slowed down and came to a stop near him. Eddie started toward it when a small figure darted before him and into the cab. It happened so fast that for an instant Eddie just stood there, staring. But when the door was about to slam shut, he reached out sharply and caught its handle.

"Don't move," he called to the driver.

"Come on, buddy, let's get . . ."

"Shut up," Eddie cut in grimly.

Then he turned away and peered into the cab. The man was small and dapper, with a thin, lean face and deep-set black eyes.

"What the hell are you trying to pull?" Eddie asked bitterly.

The man spread his arms in an uncomprehending gesture. "Señor?" The voice was soft and melodic. But the eyes were sharp and wary.

"Get out."

"Hurry, Señor. In hurry."

"I said, get out."

"Please, Señor. Hurry."

"Come on, let's get going," the cab driver broke in angrily.

The words and the voice set Eddie off. It was all the spark that he needed. "I said shut up, you sonofabitch!"

He turned back with fury to the small, dark man. "Goddam you, get out."

Before the man could say anything, Eddie reached in and grabbed him, lifting him out and setting him down hard on the sidewalk.

"Please. Please," the man protested.

"The hell with you," Eddie said.

He got in and slammed the door shut. The cab started up.

"Señor! Señor!!"

The little man frantically tried to open the door.

"Get going," Eddie said to the driver.

As the car swung away into the traffic, Eddie turned and looked back. The man was out in the street running after them, his hands waving wildly. Eddie kept looking till the desperate figure was lost in the distance.

"East Eighteenth Street. Between Second and Third Avenue," he ordered the driver.

"Okay."

It was then that Eddie felt the brief case at his side.

"The guy sure wanted a cab bad," the driver said.

"Just keep driving," Eddie said. "I don't like the way you talk."

"I just wanted to get going, that's all."

"You almost got going, man. Right on your ass."

The driver was silent. Eddie turned his attention back to the brief case. Its lock gleamed in the dimness of the cab. The leather felt soft and smooth. Eddie's big hand stroked it thoughtfully.

I guess it belonged to the little Spanish guy, he said to himself. I didn't see him get into the cab with it. But, come to think of it, I almost didn't see him get in until he was in.

His hand stroked the leather, measuredly, rhythmically.

"East Eighteenth Street?"

"Yeah."

Eddie lifted the brief case and then set it down again beside him. It was heavy. He thought of the little man and how he had run into the street after them, his arms wild with loss.

He began to feel sorry for what he had done.

The brief case must mean an awful lot to him, he thought.

"Turn around," he suddenly said.

"What?"

"Turn around and head back for Eighth Avenue."

"Okay."

"Right where you picked me up."

"Whatever you say."

While they were riding, Eddie kept staring at the little brass lock of the case. There must be some important business papers in there, he thought. That's why the little fellow had the lock on it. Must be pretty important to him. Maybe he was in a bastard hurry to get to some important appointment. Maybe he was scooting for a plane at the airport.

Then he'd have other bags with him.

"Here's where I picked you up," the driver said.

Eddie shoved the brief case into the shadows of the seat and got out of the cab.

"Just stay put till I come back."

"You didn't pay me yet."

"I know. That's why you'll stay put."

Eddie smiled coldly at him, turned and scanned the crowded sidewalk. There was no sign of the little man. He walked slowly up and down the long block, his gray eyes searching out every passing face, every hurrying figure. After a while he sighed and gave it up.

The man had vanished.

"All right, you can take me back now."

"East Eighteenth Street?"

"You got a good memory. You should be on a quiz show."

"You still don't like me?"

"That's right."

In the days to come Eddie would think back about that, wondering how things would have turned out if he had liked the cab driver. He would have given the brief case to the driver and it all would have ended there.

Ended.

And no one would have died.

But he didn't like the driver, and so, he didn't trust him with the case.

"You look familiar to me," the driver said.

"Do I?"

"You're a fighter, aren't you?"

"I was."

He would wonder. Wonder why of all the cab drivers in New York he had to fall in with this one. And in the end he would say to himself, with a broken cry, Fate! And let it go at that.

"Didn't I see you at Saint Nick's? About four months ago?"

"No."

"Yeah. You're Eddie Doran, aren't you?"

Eddie tucked the brief case inside his overcoat and sat back against the seat again.

"Sure, that's who you are. You were real good, Eddie. Didn't you once go a split decision with Archie Moore?"

"That was a long time ago."

"Not so long ago. I remember seeing it on television. You were out in Chicago. Wasn't it there?"

Eddie didn't answer.

"A great fight, Eddie. You shoulda had it. Great fight. About eight years ago. Seven or eight years ago. In the summer. Right, Eddie?"

"A hundred years ago," Eddie said. Then he added quietly, "I said you talk too much."

The driver was silent until they pulled up in front of an old apartment building. It loomed dully in the night, flanked by shabby brownstones. The block was windswept and deserted.

"This where you want to go?"

"Yeah."

"Sorry I rubbed you the wrong way, Eddie."

Eddie got out and silently paid him. Then he stood in the bleak night and watched the car go off; its taillights flickered out into the darkness. Eddie felt alone again.

When he got upstairs he sat around the small dreary apartment for a long while. The wind was getting stronger, pushing hard against the windows. Eddie went into the kitchen and took a screw driver from one of the cupboard drawers.

Setting the case on the table, he began to work at its lock. The picking sound of the screw driver mingled with the rattling of the window panes. Finally the brief case was open.

There was a hundred thousand dollars crammed into it.

Two

For the next three days and nights he stayed in the little apartment, only going out to pick up the newspapers. Then he would hurry back, lock the door and read through them.

There was not one word about the lost money.

On the fourth morning, after scanning the papers, he went over to the phone, stood a moment thinking hard, then slowly dialed the number. When he heard Al Walker's voice, his first impulse was to jam the receiver back onto its hook. But he didn't.

"Al?"

"Eddie? Where've you been keeping yourself? I called you a few times and didn't get you."

"Just didn't feel like answering the phone."

"Oh. You're in the dumps."

"That's right."

"You'll come out of it."

"Yeah."

There was a pause. And then he heard Al's voice again. "You call me about anything special?"

The impulse to jam the receiver came up hard again, but he found himself talking on. "Very special."

"What's up?"

"Come on over. I want to talk to you."

"I've got a few things to take care of. How about some time this afternoon?"

"How about now?" Eddie said.

There was a pause again. Then he heard Al answer. "Okay, Eddie. I'll be right over."

"And come alone."

"Why don't I take Laura along? Maybe you'll call up Carol and we'll all have a time together. Make a day of it. It'll be good for you, Eddie. Give you a lift. That's what you need, kid."

"Maybe you'll just come over alone."

There was a pause.

"Whatever you say, Eddie."

"That's what I say."

"I'll be right over."

"I'll be waiting."

Eddie hung up, went over to the window and looked out at the gray morning. The sky was grim and ready for snow; the street below was quiet and empty. A few cars straggled by and then all was silent and unbroken again.

I wonder if it's all right to bring Al into this, he thought to himself. Maybe I ought to play it all alone. I don't know. Al's got a good head on him and he's been pretty loyal through the years. We've been through a lot together and now he's almost as broke as I am. You don't find good fighters every day. And I was good, but Al helped some too.

Eddie turned away from the window and went into the dreary kitchen. He thumbed through the pile of newspapers that were on the little table, then pushed them aside, went over to the stove and lit the jet under the pot of coffee. Soon the quiet bubbling of the liquid pierced the heavy silence of the room. He stood there listening to it, thinking.

He had just finished his breakfast when the doorbell rang. Eddie sat rigid, then slowly got up and went to the door. He stood with his big body bent forward, listening, his eyes cold and sharp until he heard Al's muffled voice.

"Eddie?"

"Okay."

Eddie quickly opened the door and let Al in. Then he shut it again and leaned hard against it.

"Why the hell did you let me ring so much?" Al asked.

"Didn't realize it was ringing."

"You got ears, haven't you?"

"I got them."

Eddie kept looking at Al's face, at the alert brown eyes and the jet black hair that was just beginning to show signs of gray. The stocky, hard body in the neat-fitting suit. He knew the suit well; it had once cost two hundred dollars at Leighton's. Once, four years ago.

"You don't look too good, Eddie."

"Maybe I haven't been sleeping too good."

"Have a drink on you?"

"Yeah."

He went away from the door and over to the kitchen closet. He took out a bottle of rye. Al sat down at the table and ran his hand over the pile of newspapers.

"You going in for reading?"

"Just passing the time."

Eddie swept the papers to the floor with his big hand and set the bottle down. He put two dusty glasses on the table and sat down across from the stocky man.

"Here's luck."

"Luck," Eddie said.

The two drank silently. Al took a cigarette out, lit it and smoked steadily, his manicured nails gleaming in the thin sunlight. Outside, it had begun to snow. Soon the sun would fade out completely.

"You have much dough?" Eddie said.

Al's brown eyes bored into the big, open face. "You know I don't, Eddie."

"Just asking."

"If you need a hundred, I can give you that. But I'll be squeezing hard."

"I didn't call you here for a loan," Eddie said.

"Then why ask about money?"

"Just interested in how much you have, Al. That's all."

"You're in a crazy mood today, Eddie."

"Maybe I am."

Al's voice rose just a bit. "You know how flat I am. Whatever I made out of you went with the wind. Fast women and slow horses, isn't that what Joe E. Lewis says?"

"Uh-huh."

Eddie picked up the bottle and poured the drinks again. Some of the liquor spilled over onto the dirty oilcloth. Eddie reached his hand over and rubbed it away. "I had slow women and fast horses and still I ended up with nothing."

"You gave yours away, Eddie. Every bum come along and you gave it. I told you a million times not to."

"Drink up and shut up," Eddie said.

"At least I got fun out of mine."

"Yeah. You got fun. A whole houseful of it."

"Why is it you don't like Laura?"

"Why is it you never married her?"

Al drank and then shrugged. "Maybe because I never got around to it."

"Maybe that's why I never liked her," Eddie said.

"I don't get it."

"Someday I'll spell it out for you."

"You're in a crazy mood today."

"That's twice you said it and twice I don't like it. Lay off."

Al's brown eyes flashed ·but he didn't say anything. He waited silently until Eddie had finished his drink before he spoke. "You said it was something special."

"That's right."

Eddie sat looking at him, then slowly rose. "Wait here. I've got something to show you."

"What is it?"

Eddie's gray eyes were quiet and almost cold. "Keep your pants on."

Eddie went into the bedroom and over to the bed. He lifted up the mattress and drew out the brief case. His shadow loomed on the drawn shade.

"Come on in, Al."

He stood waiting, the brief case in his hand, a thin smile on his lips. Al paused on the threshold and then came slowly into the room.

"I found a brief case," Eddie said.

"And?"

Eddie silently opened it and dumped the money onto the white bed. It lay there in the half-light of the small room.

"Christ!" Al whispered.

"A hundred grand."

"Christ."

"A hundred grand, Al. I counted it over and over again. An even hundred grand."

Al slowly approached the money, then he stopped and stared at the big man, his mouth open. His hands hung loose at his sides.

"Like it dropped from the sky, Al. It's real. Put your hands on it and feel it. It's real as all hell."

"You found it?"

"In a cab. A guy left it there."

Al reached down and lifted some of the bills. He sat down on the bed and looked up at Eddie, his face still slack with amazement. The silence of the room hung about them.

"A Spanish guy tried to get in the cab. I threw him out. He left the brief case on the seat. You should've seen the way he ran out in the street after me. Like he had just lost the world."

Al's fingers played with the feel of the bills. Slowly, slowly. His eyes set upon Eddie's face.

"I didn't know what he was so excited about. Didn't even know the case was on the seat until it was too late."

"Too late for what?"

"To give it back to him."

"Oh?"

"Sure, I would've given it back to him."

"Yeah. I guess you would've."

Al held a hundred dollar bill in his hand, and slowly let it flutter down to the floor. He sat looking down at it, his face now quiet and absorbed.

"Yeah," he said slowly. "I guess you would've."

"I even went back looking for the guy. But it was no dice. He had disappeared."

Al stooped over and picked up the bill again. He held it close and studied it carefully.

"Looks okay to me. Although I've seen some really good counterfeit jobs."

"It's not counterfeit."

"How do you know?"

"I cashed a ten at the corner newsstand. That guy can spot a phoney bill a mile away. He's a whiz at it."

Al dropped the bill down into the pile and picked up a few more and examined them. Eddie leaned against the old dresser and watched him. Outside, the wail of a siren sounded, built up into a scream, and then steadily died away. Only the sound of Al's fingers remained. Then even that stopped. The green money gleamed dully in the shadowy room.

"A hundred is the highest. The rest is small denominations. It's not phoney, I tell you. And there hasn't been a word about it in the papers. I found it three days ago. No, today starts the fourth day." He stood there nodding his large head, and then he said, "The fourth. I've had a hundred grand for four days. It's a helluva feeling, Al. A real helluva one."

"You look in the lost and found columns?"

"I got every newspaper that's out. The Times, the Trib, the News, all of them. Not a word."

"Nothing about a lost brief case?"

"Nothing."

Al sat looking at the money and shaking his head.

"It would hit the headlines. A hundred grand lost in a cab. You'd hear it on radio, television. A guy doesn't lose a hundred grand in a cab every day."

"I've been thinking about it all the time. I can't come up with the answer, Al."

"You've been thinking about turning it over to the police?"

Eddie nodded.

"But you're not going to do it?"

"What would you do?"

Al lit a cigarette and didn't answer. A sliver of light played over the stray gray hairs of his dark head. His brown eyes were somber.

"You think it's clean money?" Eddie asked.

Al smoked silently and didn't answer.

"Why in the hell didn't the guy go to the police? That'd be the first thing he'd do, wouldn't he?" Eddie's voice became sharp and driving. "But he didn't! That's the point. He didn't. And why in the hell should I?"

"You're changing, Eddie. For a hundred grand, you're changing."

Eddie's face flushed, and he turned away from his friend's steady gaze. "Maybe I am. But I tried to find the guy. I made the cabbie go back there."

"Yeah. You told me that."

Eddie turned fiercely. "What the hell are you so high and mighty about? You'd keep the money and run."

"Maybe I would."

"Sure you would," Eddie said. "You wouldn't stick in a room for three days like you were in a cell. Thinking all the time. Trying to find the right way out. You'd just take off. Like a bat out of hell."

"If I knew I could get away with it."

Eddie turned away and went over to the window, drew the shade aside a bit and stood looking out at the falling snow. Al remained on the bed, the money about him, his eyes coolly appraising the huge silent figure.

"It's funny what a hundred grand will do to you," Eddie said bitterly.

"You're broke. It's that *and* the hundred grand. The two things come together, kid."

"Maybe."

"What did you call me up here for?"

Eddie kept looking at the steadily falling snow. He didn't speak. A thin smile played on Al's lips. "Just to show me a hundred grand?"

Still Eddie didn't speak. Al picked up a sheaf of the bills and dropped it into the brief case. The sound caused Eddie to swing around.

"Why, Eddie?"

Al's quick, alert fingers gathered up another sheaf and then held it poised over the mouth of the leather case. "Is it because you decided to keep the money and you want me to help you?"

Eddie shrugged his shoulders, his face twisted with torment.

"It's too much for you to handle, isn't it, Eddie?"

"I don't know yet what I want to do."

Al shook his head. "You know. But you don't want to tell yourself yet. That's all it is."

Slowly, steadily, Al was putting the money back into the case. Every now and then he'd glance up and note the fighter's face. When he was done he snapped the case shut and stood up.

"Okay, you want me in on it?" His voice was cool and businesslike.

"I guess that's why I called you," Eddie finally said.

"That's why." He picked up the brief case and motioned to him. "Let's go into the kitchen and talk it over. I could use a drink after this."

"I could use one, too," Eddie said, following him out of the room and into the kitchen.

Al dropped the case onto the table and sat down. He watched sardonically as the big fellow went over to the door and tried the lock.

"You locked it when I came in, Eddie."

Eddie flushed and said nothing. His fingers closed over the neck of the whisky bottle and slowly tilted it; the amber liquid spilled into the two glasses. Al held his hand up and Eddie stopped pouring.

"Luck," Al said and held up his glass.

"Luck."

They drank and put the glasses back onto the dingy table. The glasses stood like two little sentinels flanking the flat brief case, the blue smoke of Al's cigarette curling over them.

"This is the fourth day," he said quietly.

"Yeah."

"And nothing."

"Nothing. Like I picked the money out of the air."

Al's fingers drummed on the oilcloth of the table. The nails glimmered in the dimness of the room. His thick lips were pursed. Slowly he shook his head. "No hundred grand comes from the air. There's always somebody behind it. Who'd want it back pretty bad."

"But not a word, Al. Not a sign."

"Because they haven't found you yet. That's why."

Eddie breathed out low without saying anything. The glasses winked coldly. Al inhaled and let the smoke out of his thin nostrils in two sharp streams. His nose was straight and thick, but the nostrils delicate. His lips were full, almost cruel. A thin scar threaded down from a high cheekbone to his jaw. His brown eyes were somber under the overhang of the black eyebrows.

"Maybe they're not looking," Eddie said.

"They're looking."

Al reached out and struck the case repeatedly and emphatically. All the time his eyes were filled with hard thought. His hand stopped and rested, palm down on the brown leather. There was a little gold head imprinted on one of the sides of the case. Al's thick forefinger rested idly upon the tiny emblem.

"I figure it's gambling money," Al said. "That's why the police are out of it. That's why there's not a hint in the newspapers. That's the last thing they'd want is for anybody to find out about it."

"I've thought of that," Eddie said.

Al examined the little gold head. "This could mean something, or nothing."

Eddie shrugged.

"You say the guy was Spanish?"

"Couldn't speak English for beans."

"That doesn't make him Spanish."

Eddie's eyes flashed, his big face reddened. "I tell you he was Spanish."

"Okay," Al smiled. "Just take it easy. You're on edge, kid."

Eddie glowered at him silently. The shade of the narrow window rustled and was quiet again. Al reached for the bottle and started to pour whisky into his glass.

"Not for me," Eddie said. "I've had enough."

Al set the bottle back into place, then lifted his glass and drank slowly, letting the liquor roll in his mouth. The thin scar on his face deepened.

"There's a big numbers racket going on in Spanish Harlem. You know that, don't you?" Al asked.

"I know they play the numbers."

"They play it hard. Real hard."

His hand tapped the case in emphasis. "I'd say this was numbers money."

The shade rustled again and Eddie turned sharply toward it.

"It's getting cold here," Eddie said. He got up and went to the window.

"You're cold inside," Al said.

Eddie reached under the shade and shut the window tight. Then he came slowly back to the table, his eyes avoiding Al's, and sat down again. Al picked up the bottle, leaned over and poured a drink into Eddie's glass. This time Eddie didn't protest.

"You should've called me sooner. Instead of sitting here and sweating it out. You're out of rhythm, kid. Your coordination is shot. Just like you were before your last two fights."

Eddie suddenly slammed the glass down, spilling the liquor over the brief case. "Shut up. Don't bring that up. Don't ever bring that up again. That's gone. Don't get it back into my mind again. I can't take it."

"It's gone," Al said. "Forget about it."

He waited till the tautness left Eddie's face and his body relaxed again.

"But there's one thing you've got to get into your mind. If we're going to get away with this, you'd better start settling down. Otherwise we'll flop before we've even started."

And he added, "To flop means to die, Eddie. Chew on that a while." Eddie silently watched him take out a handkerchief and deftly, almost fastidiously, wipe the wetness off the brief case. Al slowly folded the stained handkerchief and put it back into his pocket.

"I say it's gambling money," Al said. "If it was robbed, the papers would've been screaming about it. It could be bookie money, but I got a feeling against that. You say the guy was Spanish, so I go along with the numbers. He could have been finished making his pickups from the different numbers banks, or just starting out to make deliveries. I'd say, with a hundred grand, he was just finished picking up."

"It makes sense to me," Eddie said.

"You got any other thoughts?"

"Just that the guy had no right to the money. Else he'd be hollering to the sky about it."

Al glanced at the brief case and then up at Eddie, a cynical smile on his lips. "He's got a right to it," he said. "Maybe the law says he hasn't. But that don't mean beans to him or the boys with him."

Eddie looked away and was silent. Then he sighed and said in a low, puzzled voice, "But there's something I can't make out."

"Go ahead."

"The way the guy acted. I know hoods. I know them long enough. You can't be a fighter without knowing them. It's the way he acted. Like he was more surprised and . . . and almost scared. Maybe not scared. I . . . I don't know how to explain it."

"It must've all happened in a flash. You say you threw him out of the cab and . . ."

"Yeah," Eddie cut in eagerly. "That must've been it. Happened in a flash. Before he knew it he was standing in the street and I was riding off. Just like that."

He snapped his large fingers and let his hand rest on the table again. His gray eyes were bewildered as he slowly shook his head. "I don't know, Al. Maybe I've been with this too long. I don't know any more where the truth is."

He got up and went to the window, lifted the shade a bit and looked out at the relentless snow. His figure towered in the small room. "Sometimes I feel like taking the money and heaving it out the window."

"Why don't you?"

Eddie kept looking at the snow and didn't answer.

"You know what's ahead of you? The nothing road. All you got are two big fists and nobody will buy them. Nobody."

Eddie's back tensed as if it had been struck. But he didn't turn. Al smiled grimly and went on. "This is the big find, don't you see it? The big find. And you and I are going to keep it that way."

"The big find."

The scar on the manager's face was now stark red. "Yes. Yes. Now tell me. Does anybody know about this?"

Eddie turned to him. "How the hell could anybody know?"

"The cabbie?"

"Not a thing."

"Good."

"Never even knew the case was there. When I got out I hid it under my overcoat."

"That's using your head. But why did you do it?"

Eddie came close to him and stopped. He stared at Al questioningly. Then he said slowly. "What do you mean 'why'?"

Al gazed up steadily, a sardonic smile in his eyes. "You didn't know the hundred grand was in the case, did you?"

Eddie shook his head. "Not till I got up here."

"But you were already hiding it. Why?"

"How the hell do I know?"

Al laughed softly and said evenly, "We all have larceny in our hearts, Eddie. Some of us hide it better than others, that's all. But it's always there."

Eddie's face flushed.

"It's there," Al said.

Eddie's voice suddenly snapped. "I didn't mean to steal it. I didn't know what the hell I was going to do with it. I just didn't take to the cabbie, that's all. That's the reason I hid it."

"Okay, if that's the way you want it."

"That's the way I want it."

Eddie's voice rose and filled the narrow room and then died away. A stillness hovered about the two of them. Finally there was the scratch and flare of a match as Al lighted a cigarette. The blue smoke wavered over the brief case.

"I figure it happened so fast the Spanish guy had no time to jot down the license number. That right?"

Eddie started to walk up and down the gloomy room, his big shadow striding along the wall. His hands hung open and slack at his sides. Al rolled the cigarette along his lips and watched him.

"Anything about the cab the guy would recognize?"

Eddie stopped by the window. The sky was like lead, the snow whirling against it.

"One of those yellow cabs. There's thousands of them in the city."

"Any marks on it? Anything that would tip it off?"

"The back fender was smashed in."

"No good," Al said. "What about the driver?"

"Name's Frank Morse. Lives over on East Eighty-sixth Street. I saw it on the hackie license."

"Frank Morse. Ever seen him around before? Around the Garden?"

Eddie shook his head. "But he seemed to know me."

"What?"

"Said he saw me fight. Knew my name."

Al slapped the case viciously. Then he ground the cigarette into the oilcloth of the table.

"That's no goddam good, Eddie. No goddam good. They find him, they find you."

He got up and went over to the sink and turned on the water hard. It thudded into the basin, its harsh sound choking the room. Then he filled a glass and drank thirstily.

"They didn't find me yet," Eddie said.

The water drummed and stopped suddenly. Al set the glass back into place and turned sharply.

"Because your luck's still holding out. It's like a dice game and you've hit a streak." The wetness glistened on his lips as he spoke, his brown eyes cold and piercing. "But streaks end, Eddie."

"They end," Eddie said.

Al's eyes flashed and his voice rose. "But we're going to keep this one going. And the best way is to get the hell out of here."

"Where?"

Al suddenly spun away from the sink and came close to Eddie. His hand gestured sharply as he spoke. "Out of the city. Any place out. South. Yeah, south. We'll fly down to Miami and stay there. The main thing is to get out. You've stayed here too long already. You should've called me four days ago."

"Four days ago I didn't know what I wanted," Eddie said.

"But now you do."

Eddie stared at the taut eager face, and then he said slowly, "Yeah, Al. Now I do."

"That's the way to talk. All right, I'll get to this Frank Morse and see that he keeps his mouth shut."

"What do you mean?"

"Money will do it, Eddie. We got money now. But we're not going to touch the big bundle yet. Let that stay sweet as it is. I'll dig into some of mine. Fair enough?"

"Think you'll find him?"

"I'll find him. Come on, let's drink on it."

He slapped Eddie on the chest and went over to the table and picked up the bottle. His hand shook as he poured the drinks. His eyes stared at the brown, motionless case.

"It's starting to get me, Eddie. I'm beginning to know what you went through, sitting here alone with all this dough."

They drank swiftly, and Eddie laughed as he set his glass down. "We'll make it, Al, won't we? It's a find, isn't it? A real find."

"You bet we'll make it, kid. Didn't I steer you right through the years? Didn't I?"

"You did, Al. You did. That's why I'm calling you in for your cut. We split down the middle, pal. Down the middle."

Al laughed and tilted the bottle again. "Down the middle. Fifty grand apiece. That's a lot of cabbage. The best purse you ever had, eh Eddie?"

Eddie grabbed his glass and drank. A thin line of sweat broke over his forehead. His gray eyes twinkled. The scar on Al's face began to look sharp and fiery. His eyes glistened.

"We'll do it, kid," Al said. "I'm going to call Laura and have her make the plane reservations. We'll hit a jet down. We'll be there in no time." He patted the big fellow and started for the living room.

"Al. No Laura."

Al stopped.

"No Laura," Eddie repeated.

"We need her; don't you understand that?"

"We don't need her."

"Are you going to let me handle this or not?"

"I don't like Laura in it."

Eddie stood, his two feet planted wide, his body swaying just a bit. But the face was cold and rigid. Al came over to him.

"Eddie, she'll never know about it. I swear to you. We're the only two who'll be in on this. That's our deal. Wasn't it always that way? Wasn't it, pal?"

"I don't like someone, I don't like someone. And that's it."

"But you can't do anything about it."

"Why not?"

"Because I just can't take off without her. I've lived with her too long, you damn fool. She'll get wise that something's up."

"No," Eddie said doggedly.

"Yes. Yes. Let me play it my way, will you, Eddie? I'll tell her we won a grand on the races and we want to go down to Miami and have a good time. Leave it to me. I know how to handle her."

Eddie turned away from him and sat down heavily on one of the chairs. He leaned forward, his eyes staring at the wall, his face still grim.

"Eddie. Eddie. Eddie, I'm no good without her. I'm leveling with you. I won't be able to think straight away from her. We'll only end up in the soup."

Eddie passed his hand wearily over his clammy face and was silent. Al came closer to him, and then rubbed his brown hair tenderly. He swayed as he talked. "Let me take her along. Eddie, we're dealing with hoods. We make wrong moves they'll cut our guts out for us. I gotta think on target

all the time. All the time. Eddie, let me take her along.
She's good luck, I tell you. She really is."

"Yeah. She's luck."

"I tell you we need her. You'll see how it'll work out.
You'll thank me for bringing her along."

Eddie kept staring ahead of him, his eyes weary and
somber.

"Eddie."

"I'm beginning to hate the money," Eddie said.

Al suddenly moved away from him and began pounding
the table. "All right, then the hell with it. I don't want it
either. If I got to ditch Laura then I don't want it. The
hell with it!" He stopped and the room was filled with
silence again. Outside the snow flaked down with a steady
iron rhythm.

Eddie looked away from the drab wall to the gleaming
brief case. "We'll take Laura," he said.

The snow flaked down.

It was just before the fall of night that Al returned.

"I got to him," he said. "I got to Morse."

"And?"

"He's in our corner."

"You sure?"

"I'm sure."

"How much did it cost?"

Al took two shots of liquor, one after another, before he
replied. "Plenty," he said.

He sat, staring at the table, his finger tracing along the
patterns of the oilcloth. There was a withdrawn air about
him, as though his mind and being were concentrated else-
where, darkly concentrated.

"Five bills, Eddie."

"Five?"

"Yeah. I told him some Spic hoods were after you. For
throwing a fight. He won't talk."

"What if they get to him?"

"They won't. He's going upstate for a few weeks. Got a
brother up there. He's taking himself a vacation. That's
why he wanted five bills."

"You look a little beat, Al," Eddie said.

"Five bills is a lot of dough."

Then he looked over to the brief case and began to smile again. There was a hard glitter in his eyes. "Hundred grand," he muttered.

His fist closed about the narrow neck of the whisky bottle. He poured himself two quick shots. Wiped his lips. "We got a hundred grand there, huh Eddie?"

"We got it," Eddie said.

"You packed?"

"Been waiting hours for you, Al."

"It took time," Al said. "Time."

Then, for no apparent reason, he began to laugh. A harsh, disjointed laugh. And Eddie thought the liquor was finally getting to him. The laughter suddenly stopped. "Come on," Al said. Let's get down to that airport and out of this murderous town."

The snow lashed like rain against the windows of the little apartment.

Three

It was while he was waiting for the plane that Eddie began reading the newspaper. The brief case lay flat on his knees. Al sat by him talking quietly to Laura. Outside, the snow was still falling.

He flipped the pages mechanically, his mind on the snow and whether it would lock them in, keep them pinned in New York till it let up. He was about to turn another page, when something within him told him to stop where he was.

Stop and chuck the paper away.

He moved his hand, as if some outer force was now in control. He turned the page.

And it was then that he saw the little notice. His face tensed as he read it.

"Lost. A brown leather brief case. In cab. Four nights ago. Near Eighth Avenue and Twentieth Street. Big reward. GE 6-7152."

Eddie sat reading the words over and over, till they began to blur before him.

Then he heard Al's voice. "What's the matter, Eddie?"

"Matter?"

"You look white around the gills."

"Oh."

"What is it?"

"Maybe . . . maybe I had a little too much to drink. It's starting to hit me. Yeah, that's what it is." But he saw Al's alert eyes fixed upon the newspaper, and he knew that he wasn't fooling him.

"Let's go and get you a bromo. That'll fix you up."

"Okay."

He slowly folded the newspaper, tucked it under his arm and got up. He looked past Al to Laura.

"Al and I had a drinking day."

"So I hear," she said.

Her face was small, with fine-shaped features. She was young looking, with a clear and fresh complexion. Her hair had an auburn tint to it. Her brow was small and smooth and very white.

"Come on, Eddie. Let's go."

"Sure."

Al turned and patted Laura gently. "You don't want a drink, do you?"

Her body was tall and lithe. She sat relaxed and sensuously graceful. Her breasts swelled hard against the tight dress.

"You don't want me to have one, do you?"

"You got the message," he said.

Laura laughed, and Eddie noted with a twinge of loneliness how appealing her voice was. Then he saw her green, cynical eyes and the twinge left him.

When they got to the doorway of the bar, out of her sight, the two stopped.

"What's the trouble?"

"Take a look at this," Eddie said.

Al took the newspaper and opened it.

"The Lost and Found column. Third item."

Eddie studied Al's face as he read the notice. There was no change of expression. He saw the cold and deliberate way Al folded the newspaper. Al handed the paper back to Eddie.

"What do you make of it?" Eddie asked.

"That they've come up with nothing. A dead end."

"Think so, Al?"

"Well, what the hell do you think?"

"I don't know."

"Eddie. Eddie, these guys run from newspapers like from a fire. Even to put a thing like this in means they're desperate. They want that money bad."

Eddie's hand tightened over the handle of the brief case, then slowly relaxed again.

"Yeah, they want it bad," he breathed.

"So let's keep away from them and get the hell out of here. That plane's got me worried. Come on, we'll go back to Laura before she starts thinking things."

"I'm just wondering if I shouldn't call the number," Eddie said. Al stared at him.

"Are you out of your mind? Let it alone."

"I'm just wondering, Al."

"I said, let it alone. What's with you, Eddie?"

"I don't know," Eddie said slowly. "Maybe I'll sleep a little better if I make the call. Maybe it's the last bit of conscience I got left."

"Eddie, you'll sleep better if you don't make that call. I got a feeling against it. Stay away from it."

"Maybe they're not numbers at all. Some guys who lost money."

"And you're losing your goddam head!"

"Maybe I am. But I just got to make the call. I got to see what's on the other end."

"No."

Eddie pushed him aside and went over to the bank of phone booths. Al swiftly followed.

"Eddie, it's a sucker move. Don't do it!"

Eddie grimly handed the brief case to him and closed the door of the booth. Al pressed close against the glass panel.

Maybe it is wrong, Eddie said to himself. Maybe the whole damn thing is wrong.

He dropped the coin into the slot and dialed. Soon he heard a man's voice. Hard and metallic.

"Hello?"

"I'm calling about your ad."

"You found the case?"

The voice had a slight accent to it.

"Maybe I did."

"Then you know what's inside."

"I know."

It was a Spanish accent. Eddie tried to picture the speaker. But all he could see was the face of the little man. The dark, wary eyes were now hard and bitterly accusing.

"Why didn't you report it to the police?" Eddie asked.

"Why didn't you?" the voice asked curtly.

"I'm asking the questions," Eddie said. "I got the case."

"You have it. And we want it back."

"We?"

"Yes."

Eddie looked at Al's tense face and said, "How much are you giving?"

"When you bring the case we'll talk about it."

"How much?"

There was a pause. Al tried to open the door of the booth, but Eddie kept his foot jammed against it. He spoke sharply into the phone. "I'm waiting."

"Five thousand dollars."

Eddie held up his hand, the fingers spread wide. Al spat viciously on the floor and tried again to open the door. Eddie kept his foot tight against it.

"No dice," he said into the phone.

"We have a description of you. You're a fighter."

"Come higher," Eddie said, and the sweat started to break out over his forehead.

"We didn't know until last night what happened to the money. The man who lost it was in a coma. He tried to kill himself."

"Are you numbers?"

"He tried to kill himself," the voice went on relentlessly, "because he knew that we would."

"Five is no deal."

"And your life? How much is that worth?"

"Five is no deal," Eddie repeated.

"I see."

The voice faded away from the phone. Eddie jammed the receiver closer to his ear and tried to listen in on the conversation that started in the dim background. He heard the word *"cinco"*, but he could make out none of the other Spanish words. The speech was too hurried and strange. Then the talk died out.

He heard the voice again.

"Ten."

"No."

"We're looking for you now. We're searching the city for you. We'll find you, we'll kill you."

"When you find me."

"Twenty."

The sweat was now pouring down Eddie's face. And he began to curse himself for ever making the call. It was like Al said, a bad move. He let the receiver dangle and held up both hands to Al. Then he dropped them and brought them up again. His lips formed the word "twenty" Al shook his head fiercely.

Eddie picked up the receiver again.

"Higher."

"What?"

"Higher."

"We'll find you," the voice seethed. "We'll find you and when we do we'll take the money out of your blood."

"You got to find me first," Eddie said.

"We will. By the time we're finished with you, you'll wish you were never born."

"Luck."

Eddie slammed the receiver onto its hook. When he got out of the booth, the sweat was running down his blanched face.

"They scared the guts outa you," Al said.

"They don't like being turned down."

"We'd better get that damned plane."

"They're after us. All the way."

"The snow's coming down too hard. Maybe that plane will never go out."

Eddie leaned against the booth. "I don't know if they're numbers. I don't know what to make of them."

"The money's not clean. They're numbers, all right, and we'd better get the hell out of town. You were a damn fool to make the call."

"I know that now. They know I'm a fighter."

"The guy told them that. Took one look at you and knew you were a pug."

Eddie wiped his big hand across his face and didn't say anything.

"You started it off wrong, Eddie. That goddam call is like a whammy."

Eddie wiped his big hand across his face and didn't say anything.

"They're searching all over town for me."

"Lots of fighters look like you. A pug's a pug."

"They're searching," Eddie said.

"So the hell with them," Al burst out. "Better start worrying about that plane. We get out of here, we're in the clear."

He shoved the brief case into Eddie's hands. "Hold on to this. I told Laura you got your scrapbook and all your clippings in here. I'm going to try to pick up a fight for you in Miami. So let's keep her thinking that."

Eddie's fingers closed possessively over the handle of the case. And for an instant he forgot the phone call.

"Laura knows how much that scrapbook means to you. You'd keep it close to you like it was your mother."

"The guy was tough, Al. Tough and hard. But he spoke good English. Like he'd had some education. Can't make him out."

"So what? Johnny Antrim was three years in college before he turned sour and went into the rackets. What are you trying to prove?"

"I don't know."

"You're rocking, Eddie. And you'd better stop it."

"I'm rocking," Eddie said.

Suddenly the voice on the public address system announced their flight.

They began to run.

Four

We'll find you, we'll kill you.

The words kept coming over and over again, strong against the steady roar of the plane.

Kill you. Kill you.

Eddie looked across the aisle at the figures of Al and Laura. Laura had her head tucked on Al's solid shoulder, her eyes closed. Her hair massed softly against his lean jaw. The dim light made the scar on Al's face look like a dull thread. Motionless, Al stared straight ahead of him.

Eddie turned back and looked out of the window into the deep well of the night. The seat beside him was empty. It made him feel more alone than ever. It would have been better if someone was beside him, just to talk away the hours. Talking keeps a fellow from thinking.

Far below, a swath of winking lights suddenly appeared. He watched it, till it was brushed away into the darkness. As if a giant hand had moved in and covered it.

We'll make you wish you were never born.

Born. He thought of the long, dreary years of knocking out a buck. It seemed to him that his whole life had been futile, to no end.

I fought my brains out and what do I come up with? I'm running like a thief in the night. All my life I tried to do the decent thing and now I'm running.

I've taken some real beatings. Some guys would find my weakness and go to work on it. Like Alcan. He crossed me up in the first round. Suckered me into a hook and had me going from there on in. I was better than him, way better, and he murdered me. I can still hear Al yelling at me to spin away from the hook. How did Alcan know I was a sucker for it? He had come up out of Mexico and I took him on for kicks. No record at all. It was kicks and a buck. But the guy beat me.

Al and I had a helluva argument over that fight. He claimed I never listened to him. But what was there to listen to? The guy knew and suckered me. How did he know when he never saw me fight before?

That's the way it is with some fellows. They're able to size me up. Maybe that's why I never went farther than I did. I'd go along okay and then I'd come up against one of these cuties like Alcan, and get taken.

Is this Spanish hood the same way? Will he be able to sucker me somewhere along the line, like Alcan did?

The phone call was a sucker ·move. I didn't even know the guy and already I made a sucker move.

We'll take the money out of your blood.

Blood.

Alcan. The poor bastard had to go and get himself killed in the ring. So I gave his wife and kids four grand. Maybe if I had that four grand today I wouldn't be on this plane. Al says we all have larceny in our hearts. I don't know if I buy that. I never had it in me before.

But it's there now. It's there now.

He turned away from the window and glanced down at the empty seat beside him. Then he heard Al's voice.

"How's it going, kid?"

"Okay."

"Stop thinking so much. Relax."

"Uh-huh."

"It's a good flight."

"Yeah. A smooth one."

Al winked at the brief case on Eddie's lap. "Smooth," he said.

"Right."

Al turned his head away, leaned closer to Laura, and shut his eyes. Eddie sat watching the two, till the stewardess came up the dark aisle and paused at his side.

"Still awake?"

"Yes."

"Would you care for some coffee?"

"No, thanks."

"Everything all right?"

"Fine. Just fine."

She smiled pleasantly and went on, but her scent remained, starting a sharp yearning within him. His gray eyes filled with the pain.

I'm lonely as hell, he said to himself. All the years and all the girls, and I'm lonely as hell. Alcan had a wife and kids, at least he had that. So his life amounted to something when all is said and done. Even Al there has something.

No, he's got nothing. They live together and come up with nothing. Maybe that's why I have no use for her. I can't see a girl waste her good years on an arrangement like that. Either you go all the way and settle down and have a home and kids, or you call it quits from the beginning.

That's one thing about Al that always grated on me. He can be a taker when he wants to. He'll take what he can, all he can, and then he'll go on. When he's through with her, he'll go like the wind.

But that's not all of Al. No. I wouldn't't've stayed with him all these years if that was all the guy was. He's been decent to me down the line. I never had a pal like him. Al understands me and I feel right with him. And he's been pretty good to Laura. That's one thing about him, he never two-timed her. Never denied her anything. She's his girl and there's nobody else.

He was willing to give up the deal for her, wasn't he?

Yet, sometimes, he's a hard guy to read. Sometimes I wonder if I can read him at all.

The plane suddenly hit an air pocket and rocked violenty. The brief case slid from Eddie's lap and onto the floor. A hot, fearful flush went through him as he swiftly bent to pick it up. Only when the handle was back in his tight grip again did the scared feeling leave him.

"Got it, pal?"

Eddie nodded. Al smiled and closed his eyes again. His face became dull and slack, as if in sleep. Yet Eddie felt that beneath the closed lids the eyes were ever alert, ever awake.

He's in on the dough, and he'll want his full cut. I guess that's why I couldn't turn the money over even if I wanted to. Al is going to get his fifty grand, come hell and high water. I guess there's no backing out anymore. Even if I wanted to.

"Eddie?"

Al came over to him and sat down in the empty seat. Eddie waited for him to speak again.

"I've been doing a little thinking," Al said in a low voice. "About this baby."

He tapped the brief case.

"We're going to ditch it," he said.

"What do you mean?"

"Just what I said. We'll take the dough out and put it in a vault. And get rid of this."

"In a vault?"

"One of the banks on Lincoln Road will be okay. We'll do it the first thing in the morning."

"I never even put anything in a vault. I don't know how you go about it."

"Because you never had anything to put in. No jewelry, no important documents. That's what people put into vault boxes."

"I don't know," Eddie said. "I just don't like the idea of carrying the stuff into a bank. I got a feeling I'll never get it out again."

"The safest place to put it, Eddie. You going to carry this around with you all the time? You can't leave it in the motel room, can you? You saw the way it dropped to the floor before. Too damn risky."

"I've been thinking about that," Eddie said slowly.

"You got any better ideas?"

"No."

"Then it's settled. We'll go down in the morning and take care of it."

"How does it work?"

"You get a box and a key. Any time you want you can go to the box. With the key."

"Who keeps the key, Al?"

"The guy who puts the dough in. That's the way it works. Nobody else can use the key."

"I don't like going into the bank with all that dough. I'll make a wrong move. I don't like it."

"There's nothing to it, Eddie."

"I still don't like it."

"All right, then I'll do it."

Eddie was silent.

"Got to be done, Eddie. You're not carrying around a bag of paper."

"It's not paper," Eddie murmured.

"Well?"

"I always trusted you, Al."

"We wouldn't be on this plane if you didn't, Eddie."

Eddie looked out at the wall of darkness. It seemed to press in on him. His hands clenched and slowly opened again. The big fingers rested slackly upon the smooth brief case.

"All right, Al," he said. "You can have the key."

Their eyes locked. Then Al got up and went back to his seat. The plane went on, piercing the black night, like a deadly sword.

Five

He waited for Al to come up the stairs from the shadowy vault room. There was a tightness in his chest, hard and stifling. And a feeling swept over him that unseen eyes were watching him. Watching and noting everything. Eddie's face was drawn with anxiety.

He longed for the reassuring sight of Al's solid figure. The more he waited, the more his anxiety grew.

Then he saw her.

She was standing across the wide terrazzo floor, at one of the glass-topped counters. Her back was to him, her dark shining head inclined. A burst of sun came through the bank window and onto the tall, slim figure. Her dress was white and shimmering in the light.

Eddie hesitated, then turned and slowly walked across the floor, till he was near her. His eyes studied the absorbed face, the clean, delicate profile, the black, glistening hair.

She stood unaware of him, busy with the deposit slip that she was filling out. He gazed at the sparkling olive skin, and then said, "Mia."

She slowly turned and looked up at him.

"Mia Alvarez?"

"Eddie? Eddie Doran."

"That's right."

The pen clattered onto the glass and lay still. Her dark, liquid eyes laughed. She put her hands out and grasped his. It sent a tremor through him.

"Eddie Doran. What are you doing down here?"

"Just down."

"A fight?"

He shook his head and smiled; her hands still lingered upon his. He stared at the dark beauty of her face. He felt a sudden aching hunger well up within him. But his voice was gentle.

"That's all done with, Mia."

37

"I'm glad, Eddie."

"It's done with." ˉ

He reluctantly let go of her hands, but their touch still lingered with him.

"It's a long time since we saw each other, Mia." A shadow flickered over her eyes. "A long time."

"You were just a kid then. I'd say no more than fifteen, Mia?"

"I always looked younger than I was, Eddie. And Father was always older than he claimed to be."

He nodded. "I never knew till a little while ago that Joey was six years older than the records show. One of the fight managers told me."

"Yes, Eddie. Father changed his name from Alvarez to Alcan when he came to this country. It helped cut the years away. And get him more fights."

"Joey was good. Real good."

"He was a good man," she said, and her voice trembled.

He didn't say any more. Then he felt her touch him again.

"Mother keeps saying prayers for you, Eddie. We've never forgotten what you did for us."

"It was nothing."

"It was everything."

"Forget it," he said gruffly.

She shook her head. Her face was now tender and glowing. "I've often thought of you. Eddie. It's not forgotten."

He flushed and shrugged his big shoulders. Then he said, "How're they making out?"

"Struggling along. The family's in Mexico City. I live here."

"How long?"

"Five years."

Eddie's response was stupid with surprise. "Five? I've been down here ten, twenty times. Never saw you."

She laughed, a low melodic laugh that rippled through him. "Miami's a big town, and maybe you never looked in the right places. I'm a librarian. I work just over the Causeway in Miami."

"I don't go to libraries much."

Again she laughed, and he noted how the slim body quivered in the white, sparkling dress.

"Maybe you should."

"That an invitation?"

And he was surprised at himself for saying that. An amused twinkle came into the dark, liquid eyes.

"If you want it that way?"

He flushed again, then said awkwardly, "I ... I guess I do."

"Fine. The hours are nine to five. Come in any time you wish."

He was about to speak when he became aware of Al standing by them. In his hand was the brief case, flat and empty. Eddie tightened involuntarily.

"Ready?" Al said, not even noticing Mia. It was as if she weren't standing there.

"Yeah."

"Let's go."

"You remember Mia, don't you?"

"Can't say I do," Al said curtly.

"Joey Alcan's daughter. The only one he had."

"I don't believe we ever met," Mia said.

She glanced at the brief case and then at Al. He stared coldly at her, then muttered, "No. We never did. Let's go, Eddie."

"So long, Mia," Eddie said.

"So long, Eddie."

When he was outside, he turned furiously to Al. "What the hell did you have to give her the cold treatment for?"

"What the hell did you have to start talking to her for?"

"She's Joey Alcan's daughter."

"I know that."

Al walked over to the car they had rented and got in. He left the door open for Eddie who followed sullenly. The motor started up angrily and they drove away, the empty brief case on the seat between them.

Al broke the silence. "I know she is. And her name's Alvarez. That mean anything to you?"

"No."

Al swung the wheel hard and headed for Collins Avenue. The sun glared down on the two of them.

"It's Spanish, you jerk. Stay away from that. She saw me with the case. Stay away from her."

"So she saw the case. So what. What the hell does she know what it's all about?"

"She's Spanish. And for a hundred grand I don't trust anybody with a Spanish name."

He hit the horn hard, again and again. Its sound blared out against the clear sunshine. There was no one in their way.

"I don't like her being there when I come up from the vault. I don't like the goddam telephone call you made. I don't like the way it's all starting out."

"Stop hitting me with that telephone call."

"It was a crazy move to make."

"I'm a crazy guy."

"All right, crazy guy. Stay away from her. I know you'd like to bang her, but stay away."

"Shut up, Al."

"You'll get a knife in your gut yet. I don't trust anybody with a Spic name, do you get me? You'll stay at the motel and keep away from town. Just keep away."

The sweat was pouring down Al's face. "The money's in a grave now. I got a feeling that before we get it out again there's going to be some dead bodies lying around."

"Now you're the one who's talking crazy," Eddie said.

"I got a feeling."

When they came to the motel, Eddie went into his room and slammed the door shut.

For a long time he stood motionless, thinking.

Six

He sat on a chair and gazed through the window out at the ocean. The sun was low and dying; it threw its last red gasp out over the sky and onto the wide water. There was quiet and stillness over everything that his eyes looked upon.

A vast, deadly stillness.

Far, toward the rim of the ocean, he saw the burnished sail of a small fishing boat. It hovered and gleamed and fell out of sight. A bird suddenly winged before him. Caught in the red glow, it veered gracefully and vanished.

He sat there watching till the sky darkened. It was then that he heard the door open and quietly close. He turned and saw the figure of Laura standing in the gloom.

She had just come out of the pool, and her bathing suit was wet and glistening.

"Eddie?"

"What do you want?"

"Mind if I come in?"

"You're in."

She came over and sat on the bed across from him. A bit of light left in the room fell faintly over her lithe, wet body.

"You're getting the bed wet."

"It'll dry."

"Yeah."

"You're in a bad mood, Eddie."

"I'm always in a bad mood when you're around."

"Why?"

He looked into the darkening ocean. A soft wind had come up. Far out, near the dead horizon, whitecaps began to show. Soon the wind will rise, he thought, and the surf begin to pound.

"Al went downtown to pick up some papers."

"I know that, Laura."

He heard her shift her body on the bed. He didn't turn. He looked out at the stirring ocean. Her voice came softly through the gloom to him.

"It's nice down here, isn't it?"

"Uh-huh."

"What's he so interested in papers for?"

"I guess he likes to read."

She didn't speak for a while. The thin light faded out of the room and they sat silently in the darkness.

"It's cozy without lights, isn't it, Eddie?"

"Sometimes I like it that way."

"Is this one of the times?"

"What do you want, Laura?"

"Just felt lonely and thought I'd talk to you, Eddie."

"I see."

"You got a cigarette, Eddie?"

"There's a pack on the bureau."

"Mind if you get it for me?"

"I mind."

"Will you, Eddie? Please?"

He got up slowly and stared through the darkness at her. He could see the whiteness of her arms and legs, her face.

"I'm tired, Eddie. The swim knocked me out."

His hand fumbled along the bureau top till he found the cigarettes. Then he went over to the bed and stood by her. He could see her lips smiling up at him.

"You're a doll, Eddie. Thanks."

He dropped the pack and matches onto the bed and then went back to his chair.

"I thought you'd sit here a little while and talk."

"What are you trying, Laura?"

"Nothing. Do I look like I'm trying something?"

He didn't answer. Soon the flare of a match broke the darkness, and he saw her face light up, the eyes gleaming.

"What's with you two guys?"

"What do you mean?"

"There's something about the way you're acting that just doesn't add up."

"You think too much, Laura."

"What is it, Eddie? Why did you register under different names?"

"Al's trying to get me a fight. Nobody'd use me under my real name."

"What did you go downtown this morning for?"

"To count marbles."

She laughed softly and he heard the rustle of the suit as she shifted her body on the bed.

"Watch out you don't set fire to the bed."

"I'm careful. I'm always careful, Eddie."

His jaw muscles twitched. He heard the slow, soft rustle again and the sound of the suit straps as she slipped them over her shoulders and down.

"Eddie?"

"What?"

"Why don't you like me?"

"What are you doing there, Laura?"

"Taking my suit off."

Then he heard the suit drop to the floor.

"What's with you fellows, Eddie?"

"Get out of here, Laura."

"Something's up, isn't it, Eddie?"

He stood tautly in the darkness, looking away from her naked body. Ahead of him the surf began to pound.

"Al's a funny guy, Eddie. You never know when he'll pick up and run. You're not that way, Eddie. You're the loyal kind. Once you like a person you stick with them. Isn't that so, Eddie?"

He heard again the shifting of her lithe body. He heard the sound of her fingers tapping out the cigarette.

"What is it, Eddie?"

"I told you it was nothing, Laura."

"What's he looking for in the papers? What's with the brief case you took this morning?"

He heard the sound of her feet softly touching the floor.

"Laura, get out of here."

Then her soft approach.

"It's something, isn't it, Eddie? There's dough in it somewhere. It must be a lot or you two wouldn't be acting this way. Like a couple of hoods that just pulled a job."

"Damn you, Laura, it's nothing."

He heard the soft laugh again. It was close to him. Almost upon him.

"It's everything, Eddie."

She suddenly pressed her body to his; the touch of her breasts flared through him. He began to kiss her.

And as he did, he knew it was wrong, desperately wrong, that he was losing something, something he would never regain.

"Hold me tighter, Eddie. Tighter!"

He kissed her again. His hands moved fiercely over her thighs, his lungs gasped.

"Eddie, Eddie, you're better than him. Better!"

"Laura."

"Bett . . . er," she panted. "Bett . . . er."

Her teeth bit into his shoulder, and she began to moan. Over and over again.

Till her body began to move with a spasmodic rhythm.

"Soon, Eddie. Soon!"

His passion rose to a white searing pitch.

But deep in its core was a cry, silent and fearful.

Seven

"All right, Laura. You'd better go now."

"Eddie."

"Come on. Al will be back soon."

"We still have time. Don't you want to try it again, Eddie?"

She leaned over upon him, her breasts rubbing softly against his bare chest. Her hand stroked his leg.

"Just once more, Eddie?"

He pushed her away from him and sat up in the bed. "You've just got time to get back to your room. So get going."

"Can't we talk a little then, Eddie?"

"Laura, for crissake, will you stop it?"

"You're getting angry at me, Eddie. After you've been so nice. Didn't you love it, Eddie? You acted like you did, Eddie."

"Laura."

She laughed low, let her hand pass over his flat, hard stomach, laughed again as he quivered, and then got off the bed.

"You never liked me before, did you, Eddie?"

"Get the suit on fast, will you?"

"Will you help me?"

"No."

The moon was up. Its rays filtered into the room and onto her gleaming body. He thought how beautiful she looked then, like a silvery animal. How beautiful and how deadly.

And he understood then why he had never liked her. Because he feared her.

"We'll do it again, Eddie. The next time will be more thrilling. The more we get to know each other, the more we'll love it. It always works out that way, doesn't it?"

He watched her slip one shining leg and then the other

into the glistening suit, slowly draw it up, till she came to her white shapely breasts. Her hands cupped them from underneath, lifting them high and firm.

"Would you like to kiss them once more, Eddie?"

"Get out, Laura."

"Don't you like to be taunted, Eddie? Most men do."

She came closer to him and then suddenly stopped and began to laugh. Her hands dropped away and the breasts rippled as her sharp laughter filled the room.

"You're like a kid, Eddie. You want the apples and yet you're afraid to reach for them."

"And you're like a whore, Laura," he said quietly.

Her laughter stopped dead. Her face became cold and hard. She stared at him, the green eyes flashing. Then she silently drew the rest of the suit up and over her breasts.

"Maybe I am," she said. "But you shouldn't have said it."

Then she went swiftly out of the room.

He was sitting at the window, staring out at the night, when he heard the door open; he thought it was Laura again. But when he turned he saw the solid figure of the manager.

"Eddie?"

"When did you get back, Al?"

"A few minutes ago."

"Oh."

"What the hell you sitting in the dark for?"

"Just sitting."

"Let's put a little light on the subject, pal?"

"Go ahead."

Al snapped on one of the lamps and a glow spread through the room. "That better?"

"Yeah."

"Draw the curtain. Let's have a little privacy."

Eddie rose and pulled the curtains. He sat down on the bed and reached to the little night table for his pack of cigarettes. He noticed a butt with a ring of lipstick on it. His hand closed swiftly over the ashtray. His eyes darted over to Al. Al sat absorbed, thumbing through one of the newspapers he had carried in with him.

Eddie dropped the butt onto the floor and kicked it under Al's foot. And as he did that, he felt like a thief.

It was not a good feeling to him.

"Want to show you something, kid. Ah, here it is."

Al came over and sat down on the bed beside him. Eddie lit a cigarette and then took the newspaper from Al.

Al spoke. "Been in my mind like a nail, ever since you made that bastard call in the airport. Read the notice there, boy. It's good reading."

"Over here?"

"That's right."

"It's the New York *Times*. Today's paper."

"You still can read," Al said drily.

"Two words at a time."

He read the notice aloud. "Regarding the brief case. We will come to terms. Contact us. You know the number."

Eddie slowly put the newspaper down.

"That means they found nothing, kid. They still think we're in New York."

"Yeah."

Al slapped him on the shoulder. "That all you can say? Those jokers are running around in circles. If they're raising the ante that means they know they're on the losing end."

"That's right."

"Right? That all I hear from you? We're sitting here in the sun and they're looking their eyes blind up there in the snow. Did Uncle Al make a good move or not?"

Eddie kept thinking of Al sitting on the same spot where Laura had sat. "It was a great move, Al. A really great one."

"Eddie, wake up, will you? You know, after you made that jerkoff call you had me going. That was one of the reasons I decided to run the money into a vault box. I started seeing Spanish hoods all over the place. I started thinking maybe they'd trace the call. Maybe hear the noises of the airport through the phone. Maybe recognize your voice. Crazy things like that. You had me going, Eddie."

"I sometimes think crazy things too, Al."

"Then stop. And stop making stupid moves again. You got to keep a clear head."

Al grabbed the paper out of Eddie's hand and flung it to the floor. "Clear head, Eddie. There's your proof. They wouldn't be putting ads in papers up in New York. And a real desperate one like this. 'Come to terms.' They're hanging with their tongues out. They see that money flying away, like smoke."

Eddie breathed out sharply, then turned to Al and said, "Why don't we come to a deal with them, Al?"

Al stared at him, his mouth dropping open.

"Maybe we'll be able to get forty grand from them. Isn't that enough for us?"

"You out of your mind?"

"Isn't it, Al?"

Al swung off the bed and stood up. The lamp light caught his black hair and gave it a hard sheen. The scar on his cheek reddened.

"What's with you, Eddie?"

"Nothing."

"It's something."

"Just that I feel we should come to a deal."

"You said that."

Eddie shrugged and was silent. He wanted to rush from the room and into the shower and wash Laura off from him. Al's brown eyes studied the big, troubled face. He suddenly began to shout.

"What the hell is it, Eddie? What?"

"Who knows?"

"I know. Even if it isn't a trap, I know we're not giving up a hundred for forty. Not as long as I live."

"A trap?"

"You poor dumb pug. They're not going to give up forty thousand easy. I know these guys. This is their move to set a trap. Just trust me and forget it."

"Okay," Eddie suddenly burst out. "You won your point. Forget it."

"Okay. It's forgotten. You never said it."

"I never said it," Eddie snapped out.

Al sighed heavily and sat down on the chair. His face was pale and moist, his breath short and hard. Eddie lit a cigarette and smoked sullenly.

After a while, Al said, "I dropped the brief case into Indian Creek."

Eddie didn't speak.

"Put some rocks in it and dropped it down. It's on the bottom now."

"It was only a brief case," Eddie said. "What did you go to such trouble for?"

"Just felt it was best to get rid of it. That little gold head on it got me going. Could be a tip-off. Had a feeling about it."

"You swing high, you swing low," Eddie said.

"What do you mean?"

"What about the feeling that the money was in a grave? The dead bodies?"

"That was before the ad, Eddie."

"It could be a sucker ad."

"I tell you we're in the clear."

"You swing high, you swing low."

Eddie crushed out his cigarette and got up. "I think I'll take a shower." Then he added, "I got a feeling there will be dead bodies before we're done. Our own."

Al got up.

"Our own," Eddie said.

"All right. All right. This used to be an easy state for guns. I don't know how it is now. May take a little while but I'll pick up two for us. Will it make you sleep better?"

"No. I don't like guns, Al. I don't like what they mean."

"Just for bluff, kid. You listen to your old manager. Okay?"

· Eddie shrugged and went into the bathroom. He stood in the darkness a long time before he finally turned on the light.

Eight

He was lying alone on the sand under the shade of a solitary palm tree, when he felt that someone was standing near him. The shadow fell sharply across him, covering him with a strange, unreasoned terror.

"Hello, Eddie."

He stared at the slender figure in ·white, at the dark, luminous eyes. And the terror slowly crept away, like a mangy cat. And all the time she was with him, it remained in the dim, tangled background, ever there.

Strange and unfathomable.

"Surprised? You look it."

"Mia."

He watched her sit down beside him. Her scent, different from Laura's, from that of any woman he had ever known, hovered delicately about him.

It was plain, it was exotic, it was sophisticated; it was coarsely passionate.

"It's three days, Eddie. I've been waiting for you to come to the library."

"I . . . I just didn't get around to it."

"Oh?"

She leaned her back gracefully against the scored trunk of the tree, then took off her wide-brimmed straw hat and set it down beside her. The breeze strayed wisps of her dark, shining hair.

"Maybe you never intended to."

"No, Mia. It's not that at all."

"Then what?"

"Just worked out that way, that's all."

"But you would have come?"

"Yes. I've been thinking of you an awful lot."

She touched his muscular arm with one of her tapering fingers and he felt his body thrill.

"Do you expect me to believe that?"

"Yes."

"You lie beautifully, Eddie."

"Mia."

"Don't plead with me, because it's of no use. I just won't believe a word you say."

"Okay, so you won't believe me," he grinned.

She laughed, her white teeth flashing against the olive skin, the dark eyes dancing. He watched her and felt a dull ache begin within him. He looked away from her to the sparkling ocean.

The sky was massed high with towers of shimmering clouds. Then he heard her soft voice again.

"Aren't you wondering how I found you?"

He turned slowly back to her. "I was."

"But you didn't say anything."

"Just wondering, that's all."

"You're a strange person, Eddie."

He waited silently while she lit a cigarette, noting that her nose was just a little too long and straight. He saw the sheen of her dark, smooth hair. The small, narrow brow. The smoke curling up from lips that were a bit too wide for the face, and yet seemed right. So right.

"I'm a very systematic person, Eddie. Most librarians are, or didn't you know that?"

"I told you I don't go into libraries much."

"Yes, you did."

Her eyes were gentle as she said, "I knew that you were in Miami Beach. I knew that you'd be staying at one of the motels."

"Why not one of the hotels? There are a lot of them here."

She smoked lazily and gazed out at the quiet, green ocean. "I thought about that a long time. I decided you would prefer the more informal life of a motel."

She turned her eyes gently, appraisingly upon him. "Was I right?"

He didn't answer.

"Then it was a matter of driving from motel to motel until I found the right one."

"I'm registered here under a different name, Mia."

"I told you I'm systematic. I'm also persistent."

Her laughter suddenly rippled out. She leaned over and took his hand in hers. "Eddie, if you could see yourself now. Your face is so serious. Why?"

He felt her warmth throb through him. He slowly let go of her hand and smiled. "I guess it's the big dumb look I always carry around with me. It's from being hit too much up here." He tapped his head and grinned at her.

Mia shook her head. "Don't ever speak like that again, Eddie. You have a good face. A handsome one."

"Yeah."

"You have, Eddie."

His big hand lifted up some sand and let it sift through the thick fingers. "When I was a kid," he said, "I had a pretty straight-looking face. But that was more than a hundred and twenty fights ago."

"Eddie," she said and her voice quivered.

"Sure, I don't look like some of the other guys do. I'm not carrying around two tin ears and I can still see through my two eyes. I don't shuffle along like a stumble-bum, but I know how I look."

She bent over to him, kissed him on his cheek and then drew quickly back.

"Don't ever speak like that again, Eddie."

"Why did you do that, Mia?"

"I've been wanting to do it for a long time."

"A long time?"

"Ever since you came to us with the money."

He felt the ache begin again inside him, and this time there was bitter disappointment mingled with it. He groped for the feel of the dry sand.

A pink flush had come to her smooth cheeks. "You're like a child," she sighed. "A big child."

"Why, Mia?"

"Someday you'll understand why."

"I don't get it."

"I know you don't."

She lifted her hat from the sand, and he thought with a sudden stab of fear that she was leaving him. Then she brushed the brim with an almost delicate motion, her eyes twinkling at him, and set the hat down again.

He looked away to sea again. The sun lay hot and flat upon the water, shimmering along its surface. The sky was steel blue behind the white cloud. The air hung still about the two lone figures. Behind them, in the distance, the white, low building of the motel stood motionless.

Mia broke the silence. "Where's your friend?"

"Al?"

"The man I met you with at the bank."

"He went for a ride."

"Oh."

He looked up at her. "You don't like him."

"I didn't say anything."

"But it's all there. In your eyes."

"It's not for me to like or dislike your friends, Eddie."

"Maybe it is."

She raised her slender arm and patted down the wisps of hair that the breeze had loosened. He saw the movement of her small breasts beneath the white, silk dress.

"Why did you say that, Eddie?"

"I don't know, Mia."

She smiled and patted his arm. "All right, we'll leave it that way. You don't know."

He flushed and said nothing for a while. The silence hovered about them. Then he said. "What is it you don't like about Al?"

"I didn't say that I did, or that I didn't."

"What, Mia?" he persisted.

All at once, her face became somber, her eyes cold. "I don't think the man's good for you."

"He's my manager."

"You're not fighting any more. You told me that."

He was startled at the change that had come over her. The softness was gone, and her voice had the low ring of steel to it. "Get away from him, Eddie."

"Mia."

"Get away. In Spanish we have an expression for his type of man. We call him a man of blood."

"Man of blood?"

"He's lived off your blood, hasn't he?"

"That's a hard way of putting it, Mia. And it's not right."

"But it is, Eddie. The same men lived off my father's blood. The same kind."

"Al's been decent to me all along. He..."

"He brings blood wherever he goes, Eddie. Get away from him."

She stood up, her body straight and held tightly. This time her hat was grasped firmly in her hand, and he knew that she was going. He rose swiftly to his feet.

"Mia."

"I must go, Eddie."

"Stay on, will you? Just a little longer. You come here and then you..."

She shook her head and smiled gently at him. The fierce, icy look had left her. "I have a job to take care of, Eddie. I must get back to the library."

"When will I see you?"

"When?"

"Yes."

"It was I who went looking for you, Eddie. It's not

for the woman to do the pursuing. You're old enough to know that."

"But . . ."

"Eddie. Eddie, are you that way with all women?"

She suddenly reached up and drew his head down and kissed him full upon the lips.

"Come, pursue me now."

Then she turned and walked away from him. He stood watching a long time, till her figure was lost in the shimmering distance.

After she was gone, her words struck with a chilling force.

Get away from him, Eddie. He brings blood. Get away.

It was that night, deep in the black well of the night, that his phone rang. Three different times.

And each time that he answered it, there was no one. Only silence.

Nine

Eddie got out of the water, stood in the glaring sun to dry off, then went over to the shade of the tree to lie down. His huge muscled body sprawled out on the sand. His eyes closed.

The silence. The telephone calls.

Was it someone trying to work on his nerves?

The harsh ring. The lifting of the receiver off the hook, while the night hung about him menacingly.

Then silence.

Al thinks we're in the clear. The ads have stopped. They've given up.

But have they?

Or are they just starting to go to work and tear me apart. Inside and outside.

I laugh and kid around with Al in the sun. But underneath it all, are we really laughing?

I don't know what's in him. But I know what's in me. Underneath it all, I'm waiting.

The minute I found the money I knew that something had started. Something that's going to end bad. But there's nothing I can do about it. I feel myself being shoved along. And there's no stopping any more.

Not any more.

"Eddie."

He opened his eyes and stared up at Laura.

"You looked like you were dead," she said.

He sat up silently.

"Mind if I sit by you a while?"

He watched her body as it settled with an animal grace beside him. The sun glinted on her auburn hair; her small-featured face was quiet and composed. She wore a black bathing suit that hugged her supple thighs and breasts. Her skin was golden from the days in the sun.

She drew her long legs up, clasped her hands about them, and glanced at him.

"How's the water?"

"Fine. Why don't you go in?"

She laughed almost harshly, her green eyes looking steadily at him. "Why? You want to get rid of me?"

"Do what you want, Laura."

"Don't I always?"

"Yeah."

Before them was the sheer stretch of sparkling water. The ocean made a smooth line with the horizon.

"That wasn't a nice thing you called me the other night, Eddie. It keeps sticking in me. Like you put a knife there and left it."

"Let's forget that night."

She turned her head. A taunting smile had come into the green eyes. "You want to?"

He didn't answer.

"You want to but you can't. Is that it?"

"It's gone, Laura," he said. "Like it never happened."

"It happened."

He picked up a handful of sand and flung it viciously at a scurrying crab. The crab darted away, the grains of sand clinging wetly to its horny shell. Laura glanced at his drawn face and smiled.

"You're in a mean mood, Eddie."

"Where's Al?"

"Changing into his suit. He'll be along soon."

"Uh-huh," he grunted.

"He'll be along."

She sighed and lay back upon the sand. The leaves of the towering palm tree were still. Coming through them the sun fell in little shining squares upon the length of her body. Her legs lay flat, spread slightly apart.

"It's a great life out here, isn't it, Eddie?"

"Sure."

"Puts you in tune for the good things, doesn't it?"

Her eyes closed lazily, her lower lip dropped open, and he saw the flash of her white teeth. They were small and close together, and he remembered with a throb how she had bit him on the shoulder that night. And her moan as she had done it.

"What are you thinking about, Eddie?"

"Nothing."

"I'll bet it's the same thing that I am. Should I tell you?"

"No."

Her voice was low and drowsy. His eyes fastened upon the smooth-shaped legs and he felt a sudden urge to put his hands upon them and feel the warm flesh.

He turned fiercely to the empty ocean. Its soft undulant motion only stirred him more. He dug his hands into the sand and closed them tightly about it.

"You hate me and yet you want me. You want the good time all over again. Isn't that so?"

"I said forget it, Laura."

"It's easy to say, Eddie."

He looked toward the distant motel and longed for Al's figure. But there was nothing but the spread of glaring sand.

"Maybe he went into the pool. That's where everybody hangs out now. It's too hot out here on the beach."

Her eyes were still closed, her body relaxed and sure of itself. "You're an easy guy to read, Eddie. All honest guys are easy to read."

"And Al?"

"Most times you never know anything with that joker."

"Then why did you stay with him all these years?"

"Maybe I had nowhere better to go. Did you ever think of that?"

Her taunting voice cut through him. He suddenly reached out and grabbed her wrist, pulling her up to a sitting position. She twisted her body trying to get loose from him.

"You'd make a guy do anything. Even lay his best friend's girl."

"You're hurting me, Eddie."

"And then try and get him to do it again."

He fought the savage impulse to grab her to him. Grab her and fall on her, there on the empty beach with the ocean throbbing near. He leaned forward to kiss her, when he saw the key flashing in the sand.

She rubbed her wrist and watched his face as he bent and picked up the key. There was a cunning yet fearful look in her eyes.

"Where did you get this, Laura?"

He held the key up, close to her. "It dropped out of your suit."

"No. I don't know a thing about it."

"Yeah. You don't know a thing."

He slowly rose, the key gripped tightly in his fist. He breathed out heavily and stared away from her to the glaring ocean.

She stood up and came near to him. "I found it in Al's pocket."

"Yeah, you found it. After you looked for it."

He felt her hand begin to stroke his shoulder, and then the soft press of her firm breasts against his bare back.

"Eddie, I'm on your side. I told you that in the room. Didn't I, Eddie?"

He jerked away from her. "You're on nobody's side but your own, Laura."

"I just wanted to show it to you, Eddie. That's why I came out here before Al. To show it to you. It's a vault key, isn't it?"

"To show it to me and ask questions about it. Put it back before Al finds out about it. He'll break your jaw for you."

"What's in the vault box, Eddie?"

"Nothing."

She put her hand on his thigh and stroked downward. Her eyes smiled tauntingly at his flushed face.

"You'll stop fighting me yet, Eddie. Won't you?"

"You'd better put the key back."

"You shouldn't have let him put the money in, Eddie. Because only he can take it out."

"Shut up."

She laughed and held her hand out to him. He dropped the key into it.

"Eddie, he'll get up one fine morning and hike off with it. And you'll be left holding a great big bundle of nothing."

"Ditch the key before Al comes along."

"It must be a lot of money, isn't it, Eddie?"

"Ditch it!"

He watched her lift the edge of her suit and place the key between her breasts; the sun flashed over their whiteness.

Her eyes caught the yearning look in his. Her lips smiled up at him. "I was made for pleasure, that's what Al always says. What do you think? You had a taste."

She moved closer to him, and he remembered again her nakedness. The way she had made love to him, so deftly, and with such wild abandon.

"Every time Al grabs me I think of you, Eddie. You're the one whose hands are holding me."

"Laura."

She looked at his face then slowly, slowly down his body. "You're bigger than he is. Much bigger. And better."

He suddenly pulled her to him and kissed her hard on the lips. They were hot and wet and yielding. Her hands held him fiercely. A flame began in the pit of his stomach and tore downward.

"Laura."

"You should've locked the door, Eddie. You should never have let me in."

He kissed her again and again.

"Not here, Eddie. You're letting yourself go. Not here."

He slowly released her. Then he looked guiltily toward the motel. Laura laughed.

"He's not coming yet, Eddie. I've been watching all the time."

"Yeah. I guess you have."

She laughed again, moved away from him, and sat down against the tree. He stood watching her as she smoothed her hair into place. And as he watched, a feeling of fear spread over him.

I should've locked the door, he said to himself. I should've locked it. She's in my life and I don't know how to get her out.

"Eddie."

"Yeah?"

"You'd better wipe the lipstick off your face."

He rubbed his big hand over his lips, and as he did he kept staring down at her. He wondered if she handled Al as easily as she did him.

"Stop thinking about Al so much, Eddie. He's not as loyal as you believe he is."

"What do you mean?"

"He's been taking a bigger cut out of you than you think he has."

"I don't get it."

"You made a lot more money than he let . . ."

"Al never took a nickel from me that wasn't coming to him," Eddie cut in sharply. "Stop running him down, Laura."

She pushed some sand away from her legs and smiled up at him. Her white teeth glittered. "He took. The same as he's taking now. Believe me, Eddie, I ought to know."

He looked toward the motel and saw Al's solid figure step off the terrace and onto the beach. Laura followed his eyes and smiled.

"He's taking now, Eddie. The money in the vault box is yours, isn't it?"

He watched the figure slowly get larger and larger. He didn't speak.

"It was you who called him to your apartment that morning in New York. Then it must've been you who had the dough."

"You've been doing a lot of thinking, Laura."

"I've got a lot of time, Eddie."

He saw Al stop and wave his hand. Eddie slowly lifted his and waved back.

"You told him it was something special. And you wanted to see him alone. That's when I started thinking, Eddie."

"And you haven't stopped since."

"Where did you get the dough, Eddie?"

"It's only marbles, Laura. Didn't I tell you?"

"You're letting him take a cut when it's all yours. It's a sucker move."

"Then I'm a sucker."

"It's time you started taking for yourself."

"It's time you shut up, Laura."

Her face reddened beneath the tan. The green eyes flashed up at him. He studied the approaching figure and asked, "There anything on my face? Any lipstick?"

"No, Eddie. You're clean."

Their eyes met. She said in a low voice, "I'll drop into your room tomorrow. About eleven."

"Stay out."

"Eleven, Eddie. We'll do things we never did before. New things. You'll never forget them, Eddie."

Then she raised her voice and said easily to Al, "Come on over and join the party."

Al came slowly out of the sun and into the shade of the tree. He glanced at her and then smiled at Eddie. "How's it going, kid?"

"All right."

"Care for a swim?"

Eddie shrugged. "Okay with me."

"That's the spirit," Al laughed.

He reached down and patted Laura on her leg. "You stay here like a good girl and wait for us."

"I've got nowhere to go," Laura said.

He straightened up and chuckled to Eddie. "Let's go, kid."

Eddie followed the stocky body down the stretch of beach and into the water. And all the time he felt Laura's eyes on him.

"Let's swim out to the sand bar. Feel up to it, Eddie?"

"Sure."

The water was warm and soothing as Eddie stroked through it. Above, the sky was a glittering blue. The air was clean and shining. He felt the presence of Laura's eager body move further and further away from him.

They came to the sand bar and stood waist high in the water and stared about them. The day was clear and endless.

"It's a great life, isn't it, Eddie?"

Eddie nodded silently and glanced at his friend's wet, dripping face. Al brushed his hair out of his eyes and laughed up at Eddie. "We're living like kings. Like sun kings, huh kid?"

His brown eyes danced. Eddie felt a sudden warmth for the man surge over him. "It's a great life, Al," he said.

"I always told you we'd make it, didn't I?"

"You always did, Al."

Al laughed and bent and caught the golden water in his two hands. "The jackpot."

Then he flung it away with an exuberant gesture. The two laughed, their voices ringing out and then dying away. Eddie looked across the water at the tree and the small figure beneath it.

"She been giving you a hard time? She's always complaining about you," Al said.

"Yeah?"

"Says she feels you don't like her around."

"Oh."

"Makes her feel uncomfortable. Give her a break, Eddie. I know you don't go for her, but give her a break. For my sake, kid."

Eddie turned and stared at the shimmering horizon till his eyes began to smart. "How long are we going to stay down here?"

"Long as we want to, kid. Can be forever."

He put his wet hand on Eddie's broad shoulder. "You know of any better way to live?"

Eddie didn't answer. Al slowly took his hand away; the warm wetness lingered.

"Eddie, we're playing this by ear. The ads have stopped. They've given up. The money is ours."

"Is it, Al?"

But Al went on as if he didn't hear him. "We get tired of things here, we take some dough out of the box and travel a little. Rio. I got friends there. Then we come back and soak in the sun some more. What the hell more do you want?"

Eddie turned to him, wanting to shout: why did you take her along? Why? You said she was luck. Luck!

But he kept his lips clamped shut.

"You're in one of your crazy moods, kid," Al said.

"Last night my phone rang. Three times. In the middle of the night. When I went to answer it, nobody was there."

Al's face darkened.

"But I knew there was somebody on the other end."

"It's nothing."

"Maybe it's something."

Al slapped at the water and watched the spray thin out and die. "I'll be able to pick those guns up tomorrow."

"It won't make me sleep any better."

"Why?"

Eddie shrugged and was silent.

"You starting to hate the money again?"

"Maybe I'm starting to hate what money does to people," Eddie said.

Al's brown eyes narrowed. "What do you mean by that?"

"Nothing."

"What, Eddie?"

"I'm in a crazy mood. Forget it."

"Yeah. I guess you are."

They stood silently in the water. Far out, the black hulk of a freighter suddenly appeared. They watched it move slowly along the rim of the horizon.

"We know each other a long time, Eddie," Al said. "Something's eating you. What is it?"

"Forget it."

"You don't trust me with the money?"

"I didn't say that."

"You don't trust me, then we'll go in tomorrow and get it out."

The freighter veered; they watched it slowly dip and disappear over the rim. The ocean was vast and empty again.

"I'll give you your share and I'll take mine. You do with yours what you want."

Vast and empty and inscrutable.

"We'll leave it where it is, Al," Eddie said.

Ten

Eddie slept fitfully. He dreamed of one of his fights. And in the dream the face of his opponent kept blurring till it became a composite of many fighters he had fought. The body took on many arms, like a huge crab, and he didn't know how to defend himself against the rain of blows that struck him. It seemed the merciless beating would never end.

He awoke hearing the bell. His hand went to his face and he felt a thick wetness. At first he thought with a shock of terror that it was blood. Then he realized that his face was bathed with sweat.

Then the bell he had heard was that of the telephone.

Eddie sat upright in the disordered bed and stared through the darkness at the ringing phone. He slowly got out of bed and walked across the room to the insistent bell.

It was one o'clock. Eddie lifted the receiver from the gleaming cradle, and the harsh ringing stopped abruptly.

"Hello?"

Then he heard the voice and his face blanched.

"Doran?"

It had the same slightly Spanish accent. The same metallic hardness.

"Eddie Doran?"

His first impulse was to jam the receiver down and kill the voice. His hand lowered, then it slowly rose again, and he heard himself saying, "Yeah?"

"You know me."

"I know."

"I'm in Miami. I want to see you."

Eddie rubbed his hand over his wet face. Within, he felt a cold chill begin to spread.

"Doran."

"Yeah?"

"I want to see you tonight."

Eddie stared ahead of him into the darkness. The dim sound of the surf reached through the still night and into the room. With a rhythmic, heavy beat. The beat of a large and distant drum.

"Tonight."

Eddie turned frantically to the door and wondered if he should go across the corridor and wake Al. He felt weak and disorganized, as if someone had suddenly struck him.

He sought the door, as he used to seek Al's corner of

the ring when he was in bad trouble and near a knockout. It was hard to stop the thoughts that whirled through him. To stop them and concentrate upon what the voice was saying.

"I'm at the Lorraine. You'll come there."

Eddie gazed at the closed door and didn't speak. His hand lay flat and moist on his bare knee.

"Come now."

"It's late."

"Now, Doran. It's been a long search."

"You found me."

"And we should kill you now. But we'll wait. Take a good look through your window, Doran. A good one."

The phone dangled. Eddie stood in the cold shaft of moonlight, his eyes searching the motionless beach.

Then he saw straight before him two figures, sharp and angular against the night. Beyond their long shadows was the pounding ocean.

One of the figures moved swiftly forward and raised its arm. The blade of a knife flashed. It sped past Eddie, hit the wall with a spinning thud, clattered to the floor and lay still.

Eddie stood flat against the side of the window; then he reached out and slammed the window shut. His hand tore at the curtains and pulled them together.

When he picked up the knife, it felt like a piece of ice against the hotness of his clammy fingers.

Could've put it right through my gut. If he wanted to. Right through it.

He threw the knife onto the bed and went back to the phone.

"I looked," he said.

"Good."

"The Lorraine."

"You'll ask for Mr. Ferer."

"Ferer."

"We're watching every move you make. From now on in. Till we finish settling with you."

"I'll be there," Eddie said.

"You'll be there. And alone."

And then the voice became cold as steel. "The cab driver is dead, Doran."

There was a click.

He stood a long time after the voice was gone, then he slammed the receiver viciously onto its cradle. The sound crackled through the silence of the room.

Eddie opened the door and went over to Al's room. As he knocked, he looked about him, but the corridor was empty and still. Finally he heard Al's muffled voice.

"Who is it?"

"Eddie," he whispered. "Open up."

The door opened a little and Al stuck his sleepy head through and stared at him.

"I gotta talk to you. Come on."

"What the hell . . . ?"

"Come on."

The door was now fully open and he could see Laura sitting up in bed, watching them. Her naked body was smooth and silvery in the moonlight. Then the closing door shut it from view.

When they got into Eddie's room, Al turned sharply to Eddie.

"What's wrong, Eddie?"

"Everything."

He picked the knife off the bed and handed it to Al. Then he motioned him over to the window.

"The hoods," Al said and came away from the window.

"The hoods."

Eddie drew the curtains tight and went over to the lamp and snapped it on. Al's face was ashen; the scar threaded lividly down it.

"They want me at the Lorraine."

Al sat down heavily on the bed and looked dully at the floor. His eyes were dark and large.

"The guy called. The fellow I spoke to in New York. They're out for the dough, Al."

Al kept looking at the floor. "Sonofabitch," he whispered to himself. "Sonofabitch."

"They've found us."

"How?"

"Morse is dead. They killed him."

Al's hand gripped the knife tighter, but he said nothing.

"But he didn't know we were down here," Eddie said.

"No."

"But they're here."

"They're here."

He suddenly threw the knife away from him with a savage gesture. He pounded his fist on his knee, again and again. "Sonofabitch! Sonofabitch!"

The door quietly opened and Laura came into the room. They were unaware of her.

"When do they want you, Eddie?" Al asked.

"Now."

"Not wasting time, are they?"

"What do you think?"

Laura leaned against the closed door, her breasts showing through the sheer nightgown she had put on. Her small face was like a mask, only the green eyes were alive.

"They're not getting that hundred grand," Al said hoarsely. "Not if I have to kill every sonofabitch of them. It's ours, Eddie."

He swung fiercely off the bed and pounded Eddie hard on the chest. His eyes were wild and furious. And then he saw Laura. His mouth dropped open and snapped shut again. Eddie turned and stared at her.

She straightened up, taut and fearful.

"I just wanted to find out what was wrong."

"And you found out," Al said in a cold voice.

He pushed Eddie aside and moved swiftly over to her. His breath was hard and sharp. Little beads of perspiration glinted on his white forehead.

"You found out."

"Al!" Eddie shouted.

But he had already hit her hard across the face. She cried out and then fell to her knees, her breasts dropping out of her nightgown, a stream of blood flowing from her lips.

She began to whimper. The tears rolled down her cheeks and mingled with the streaming blood. Al was about to hit her again, when Eddie threw himself between them.

"Al, let her alone. For crissake, you'll kill her."

"The lousy sneaking bitch. Bitch!"

Eddie grabbed him and held him tight. "Get out of here, Laura!" he yelled.

"She knows. She knows, Eddie."

"Laura!"

He kept Al pinned till she got up and went to the door. The blood stained the lace edge of the nightgown, and he felt a great aching pity for her. But when the door closed behind her, the feeling left as swiftly as it had come. He slowly released Al.

"What the hell did you take it out on her for, Al?"

Al went over to one of the chairs and sat down heavily. The room was close and silent again.

"This is no good, Eddie. We got to think."

"Then why hit out like a crazy animal? If I didn't stop you, you would've killed her."

Al kept staring at the floor, his chest still heaving. The matted hair on it was wet with perspiration. His hands fumbled with the cord of his blue robe. "She's in now. She knows. She'll want a cut."

His fingers weaved through the blue cord, and then were still. He looked up at Eddie, a cold glitter in his eyes. "We'll take care of her later on. Now we got to think. You have a cigarette on you?"

Eddie motioned to the night table. Then he watched Al get one and light it. He shook his head when Al held up the pack to him.

"I've got a bad taste in my mouth, Al."

Al glared at him and flung the pack onto the night table.

"Thanks," Eddie said grimly.

Their eyes locked, and then Al sighed and said, "You got too thin a skin, Eddie."

"I don't like what you did to her."

Al's voice suddenly bit out. "Forget her, Eddie. We got more important things to think about. The hell with her."

Al rose and came over to him. "They're after the money and they're not getting it. Nobody's getting but you and me. That's the cut we agreed on and that's the cut we're ending up with."

He went over to the window.

"Watch out, Al," Eddie said. "Leave the curtains alone. The guy might not want to miss this time."

"They're not killing me yet," Al said.

Eddie watched the solid back become rigid.

"We'll beat those bastards yet, Eddie."

He swung around to him, his face hard as granite. "We got the dough. And it's in a box. An iron box."

"I'm going in there alone," Eddie said. "It's not a good feeling."

"I know," Al said in a low voice.

"It's an overmatch. Who the hell knows what they'll do to me tonight."

"The guns," Al said. "If I could only get to the guns tonight."

"But you can't."

"Maybe tomorrow."

"Tomorrow won't help me tonight."

Al didn't speak. Eddie started to get dressed.

"Go in and take care of Laura," Eddie said.

"Still on your mind?"

"Still."

Al patted him again and murmured. "Okay. I'll do that."

"I never saw you touch her before," Eddie said slowly. "It wasn't an easy thing to watch, Al."

"These guys got me going, Eddie. We're on the spot and they got me going. That last ad was a sucker ad. To make us feel easy and relaxed. And now they go and pull the rug from under us."

"They pulled the rug," Eddie said.

"So I let it out on Laura."

"It wasn't an easy thing to watch."

"The hell with her," Al shouted. "We're playing for our lives, Eddie."

"Not easy, Al," Eddie went on relentlessly. "Maybe that's what I meant when I said I don't like what money does to people."

Al's face reddened and he was about to speak. But he turned silently and went out of the room.

Eleven

When he got out of the car, the sultry tropic night closed about him. The air was still and heavy; the broad feathery leaves of the palm trees hung motionless. Only the sound of the ocean could be heard, boom and swish, boom and swish.

"Doran."

Eddie stopped. A man came out of the flat emptiness of the night and stood before him. He was as big as Eddie, with wide hulking shoulders and a close-cropped head. His features were thick, his nose flat and broken; the bone jutted under the skin, at the bridge.

"Well?"

Eddie saw another fellow come and stand near him. He was lean, with a narrow, angular face. Even in the moonlight Eddie could see the swarthiness of his skin. His cheekbones were high and pointed; above them the eyes stared at Eddie with a seething hatred. His hair was raven black and shining.

"You go in and you see Ferer," the big man said to Eddie.

"I know that."

"And I'm telling you again."

"Esta el hombre," the lean fellow said, and he spat into Eddie's face.

"Si, Mateo. El hombre," the big man said.

Eddie wiped the spit from his cheek, while within a hot rage began.

"Don't start pushing me around, you bastards."

"We'll push you, punk. As far as we want."

He hit Eddie hard in the jaw, then kneed him in the groin, and Eddie fell to his knees, gasping.

"Bueno, Juan," Mateo said, and he kicked Eddie savagely in the ribs.

"You sons of bitches," Eddie shouted.

He got to his feet in a fury and threw himself upon them. He hit the lean fellow on the side of the head and then spun him away from him. Then he feinted away from Juan and struck twice, two hard chopping blows. The hulking man fell flat on the gravel, the blood leaking out of his broken nose.

"Get up, you bastard, and take some more," Eddie shouted.

He stood over the fallen man. "Get up," he shouted.

Then he felt the gun barrel pressing into his back. And he heard Mateo's voice.

"Stay. You stay."

He slowly lowered his fists. But he kept them clenched till the nails cut into the skin.

"No move."

Juan got to his hands and knees, the blood still running from the wide flaring nostrils.

"Hold it on him, Mateo."

His breath heaved. He fumbled madly in his jacket pocket. Then his fist closed over a black automatic. He rose.

"I'm taking you down to the beach and giving you what's coming to you, punk."

His little eyes blazed at Eddie. The blood kept running down and over his thick distorted lips.

"Come on, punk. You're ending up in the ocean. With a bullet in your head."

Eddie stood there, rooted to the spot. An icy sensation started in the pit of his stomach and then spread rapidly through him. A cold sweat broke out all over his body.

"Come on," the twisted mouth barked. "Or I'll give it to you right here."

The gun leveled in a hard line.

Then Eddie heard Mateo's sharp voice.

"No, Juan. Ferer."

And he saw, as if in a haze, Mateo come between him and the huge man.

"Ferer," Mateo repeated.

The little eyes still blazed. But the automatic lowered and then slid back into the white jacket pocket.

"All right," Juan breathed out. "All right. But my time will come. I'll put a bullet into that head of yours yet."

He slammed his fist into Eddie's face. Eddie grunted in pain and staggered back. His hands rose instinctively, and then dropped futilely to his sides.

He felt his lips start to swell, and inside his mouth was the taste of blood.

"Get inside," Juan said. "Ferer is waiting."

Then the two of them slipped back into the darkness again.

Eddie stood there, spitting the blood out of his mouth. Then he turned and walked along the gravel till he came to the stone steps. He went up them and paused at the wooden door. His hand grabbed at the gleaming brass knocker and then rapped hard.

The door swung open and he heard the distant sound of

a lazy piano and the dim mingle of voices, coming from another part of the house. Before him was an inclined, questioning face.

"Yes?"

"Ferer."

"Ferer?"

The questioning face became a hard and wary one.

"He's waiting for me."

"Oh."

The man closed the door against the night. They went down a long bright foyer. On its pale walls were group-ings of gilt-framed paintings, all of ballet dancers in airy pinks and greys. The rug underneath his feet was thick and soft.

The man stopped before a low archway. Its columns glis-tened and Eddie touched his hand to one of them, then slowly drew it away. The sound of the piano was now clear and alive. Somewhere in the room, a woman laughed pleasantly; the laugh slowly faded into the low hum of the other voices.

"He's in there."

The room was large and dimly lit. The far end led out to a railed terrace that was but a few yards from the ocean. Eddie caught the distant sparkle of the water.

"Where?"

"The man at the table by the terrace."

"Thanks," Eddie said curtly.

A woman in an evening gown sat playing at the highly-polished piano. Her eyes casually watched him as he made his way through the tables to the end of the room.

"Ferer?"

"Sit down."

He had a long, thin body and a sensitive dark face. The nose was long and thin, the eyes deep-set and brown, the lips, narrow, bloodless, and cruel. His head was completely bald.

He studied the swollen lips and the fresh marks on Ed-die's face. He smiled thinly.

"I see you met some of my men."

"I met them."

"There are more," he said, in his hard, metallic voice. Eddie didn't say anything.

"Take a drink."

"Not in the mood."

"Take it," Ferer commanded. "What do you want?"

"Straight rye."

"Fine."

He motioned with his long thin hand to a waiter. Eddie noted grimly how quickly the waiter came running over. He sat silently watching while Ferer ordered the drinks, smoothly and crisply. The bald-headed man was meticulously groomed in a dark, closelyfitting suit, solid gray silk tie tightly knotted, and pin-striped shirt. He wore a narrow gold band on one of the fingers of his long hands.

This guy is steel, Eddie thought. Smooth as steel. The smooth side of murder. I once fought a joker like him. By the end of the fight I couldn't see out of either eye. He had sliced them open, quick and easy, like with a scalpel. I was out of the ring for six months. The worst beating of my life.

What is this guy going to do to me?

Ferer seemed to be listening to the music, unaware of Eddie. Then without turning, he spoke. "The money."

It caught Eddie off balance.

"What?"

"Did you use any of it?"

"Nothing. It's all there."

"I want it all."

"I haven't got it on me."

"I know that."

The waiter came over with the drinks. Eddie took his and drank it down. But the whisky couldn't warm the icy feeling within him.

Ferer sipped his martini. "The cab driver was found floating in the East River," he said.

Eddie said nothing.

"His head was smashed in."

"I haven't got the money," Eddie said.

"His face battered. He took a very bad beating."

In the background, the piano began again. The melody sparkled through the humming room.

"A bad way to die. There are easier ones, I'm sure."

The clear liquid in his glass shone. Ferer's lips poised above the fine rim, and then sipped again. Thin, cruel lips.

"You didn't know he was dead, did you?"

"No."

"I thought not."

His metallic voice contrasted strongly with the thin face and the lean body. The Spanish accent seemed to give it an even more menacing quality.

"You have a friend."

"Al Walker?"

"Your manager. What did he do with the money?"

"I found the money." Eddie said. "I just took Al along for kicks."

"You found the money. You took him along to manage you. To think for you. We know all about you, Doran. We know all about him."

The brown eyes became dark with hatred. The voice was edged. "We don't know quite everything yet. But we will."

"Give me time," Eddie said.

"We could torture him to death, but it wouldn't help. He loves money too much. He would prefer to die rather than give it away."

He leaned forward. "I know his kind too well. And I know your kind."

"Time," Eddie said, "and I'll get to the money."·

"You can't put your hands on it now?"

"No."

"And if we were to take you upstairs and work over you?"

"I still couldn't put my hands on it."

"My men want you killed now, Doran. Now. But they don't think. They want Walker killed. But that wouldn't help any, would it?"

"It wouldn't," Eddie said.

"Then nobody would get the hundred thousand dollars."

"Nobody."

"I thought so," Ferer said coldly.

"Give me time," Eddie said.

"Time?"

"A day. Two days. Give me two days. I'm between rounds now. I don't know how the hell to think my way out. Two days, Ferer. And you'll have the hundred grand."

He waited while Ferer sipped the last remains of the glass. Waited till the long thin hand set the glass down.

Ferer rose. His figure stood tall and dark over Eddie.

"Come with me." Ferer stood threateningly over Eddie, turned and walked to the archway. Eddie got up and slowly followed him out. As he walked, his ears kept straining for the soothing music, till they could no longer hear it.

He silently followed Ferer up a carpeted staircase and along a narrow corridor until he stopped at one of the doors. Ferer lifted his thin hand and knocked twice. The door opened.

"Get inside," he said to Eddie.

The door closed behind them.

It was a large, high room with wide windows that looked out upon the sparkling ocean. The moonlight came flooding through the windows and onto a large white bed. Two men stood near the bed. They nodded silently to Ferer and then glared at Eddie, their eyes hard and penetrating. No one spoke. The only sound was that of the implacable ocean.

The two men were Mateo and Juan.

"Come here, Doran."

Eddie approached and saw the face of the man lying in the bed, and he stopped.

"You know him."

Eddie stared at the haggard man in the bed and thought of the little fellow on the street waving frantically after the taxi.

The cheeks were now sunken and looked dark and hollow in the moonlight. The body under the sheet was quiet and small as a child's. It moved faintly with a regular but shallow breathing. The eyes gleamed and stared up at the shadowy ceiling.

The dapper little man with the brief case.

And Eddie could hear his voice like a great, empty cry.

Señor. Señor. Please, Señor. Hurry. Please!

Then he heard Ferer's voice blotting out the cry. "He tried to kill himself. He was in a coma. We've been keeping him alive until we found you. As we knew we would."

Eddie felt a chill begin to settle over him. Ferer's long lean figure looked grisly and macabre in the eerie light. When he spoke again, his teeth flashed evenly.

"We live by a harsh code, Doran. Live and die by it. No one makes a mistake and lives. Now he's going to face his mistake and die."

He turned to Juan and nodded curtly. Juan went over to the bed and raised the little man to a sitting position.

"*El hombre*," Ferer said.

The haggard face slowly swung about, till the eyes saw Eddie. Then they filled with a live and glowing hate.

"*El hombre*," the voice whispered.

The whisper was a scream to Eddie. He trembled.

"*El hombre*," the voice whispered over and over again. Till Eddie wanted to put his hands to his ears.

"Mateo," Ferer said.

Mateo took out a knife. Holding the shining blade he went over to the bed. His hair was smooth and raven black.

"What the hell are you doing?" Eddie shouted, his voice coming out choked and twisted.

Then he saw the gun in Ferer's hand and he stopped stock-still.

"Just stand and watch."

"Ferer."

"He lost a hundred thousand dollars."

"Ferer. Ferer, you'll have the money, I tell you. Let him live."

"We'll have the money."

Juan held the little man tight in his huge arms. Mateo raised his hand in a sudden sharp motion.

"Stop!" Eddie shouted.

The knife rose and fell. There was a gurgling sound and Juan let the body fall back onto the bed. A stain of dark blood spread over the silvery sheet.

All was silent in the large moonlit room.

Then Eddie heard Ferer's icy voice.

"He made a mistake, Doran. Don't you make the same."

Slowly he put the gun back into his pocket.

"Two days," he said.

Twelve

Al sat on the edge of the bed, still as a statue. Eddie started getting undressed. The room was silent except for the wind and pounding surf.

Eddie listened to it and found himself thinking of the little man, the knife plunging into his white throat and the spreading stain of dark blood.

He heard again the gurgling sound.

Eddie flung his shirt onto a chair.

"How's Laura?"

Al bit at his lip and didn't answer.

"She all right?"

"Yeah," Al muttered.

Eddie kicked off his shoes, walked over to the night table and picked up the pack of cigarettes. He lit one and watched Al's motionless figure.

"What's going to be with her?"

"Better think what's going to be with us."

"I'm thinking, Al."

"We're going to make a run for it, Eddie," Al suddenly said.

Eddie took the cigarette out of his mouth and stared at him. "I don't get you."

"There's nothing to get. The money is ours, and ours to keep."

"I told you it's a gang. Who knows how many of them there are!"

"Let it be an army, for all I give a damn."

Eddie tapped out his cigarette and came over to him. "Al, for crissake. They killed two guys already. Just because of the money. They beat me. They knocked the hell out of poor Frank Morse. What more do you want?"

"Frank Morse. He was the cab driver," Al said, and there was a bead of sweat on his forehead.

"You know goddam well he was. And they bashed his brains out. The poor bastard never had a chance. Not with those murderers!"

Eddie's voice broke for an instant. There was a hoarse ring to it. "They play for keeps," he yelled.

Al stirred himself and then snapped out, "And so do I, Eddie. So do I."

"You're out of your mind."

"Am I?"

He rose from the bed and glared at the big man. "I've tangled with hoods before and I'm still around. Did you ever know Johnny Corsi wanted in on you? Did you? When you were going good and making dough. He came to me and tried to pressure me. I'm still around."

"This is different."

"How?" Al shouted. "How? I got something a hood wants. And I don't want to give it to him. How is it different? How, you stupid pug?"

"You're rocking," Eddie said, staring at him.

"Little Spic bastards. Spic. Spic. Spic!"

Al grabbed at the window curtains and jerked them aside. His face became livid. "The hell with you, you sons of bitches," he cried. "The hell with you."

He ran to the door and swung it open. "I'll tear their lousy guts out. Nobody's getting it. Nobody." Eddie got between him and the open door. He flung Al back and closed it again.

"Cut it, Al."

"I'll kill the bastards. Kill them!"

"Al!"

"It's ours, Eddie. Ours!"

Eddie held him tight, till the wild, distracted look left his eyes. Then he slowly released him.

The manager stood there in the center of the room, his face white and clammy, a drop of spit gleaming on his lips. Then he said in a distant voice, "That's not the way."

And he said it again, as if chiding himself, "That's not the way."

"It isn't."

Al looked up at him, as if seeing him for the first time. "I guess I lost my head. Eh, kid?"

"You lost it."

"Yeah. Always the cool and collected baby. I was the one who thought out every move for you."

He drew the robe closer to his body, as though he had a sudden chill. His jaw muscles hardened. "It scares me, the way I just acted. And the way I hit Laura. Scares me, Eddie."

Eddie came over to him and put his arm around his shoulders. "It's the goddam money, Al. That's what it is."

Al's brown eyes narrowed. "It threw me for a while. But it's not going to throw me any more. I'll keep my head from now on. He nodded. "Figure out every move. Every move."

He went over to the bed and sat down again. His face was a mask. Only the eyes were alive. Like two black glittering marbles.

The room was hushed. The pounding of the surf beat against its walls.

"They gave you two days," Al said.

"Yeah."

"They wouldn't've given you two seconds. But they can't help themselves."

"I told Ferer I'd get the money."

"So you told him. The money's in a box. An iron box. Our ace card." He gripped his knee, then slowly let go. "An ace."

His eyes glittered. "We got what they want. But they can't kill it out of us." His eyes rested harshly on Eddie. "Can they, Eddie?"

"I don't like getting mixed up with a gang," Eddie said. "I don't like what I saw tonight. I don't like what I got."

"You had a rough round," Al said. "You had rough rounds before. I told you it was numbers way back in New York, didn't I?"

"Maybe I didn't think it through then."

"You mean maybe you weren't scared then."

Eddie's lips thinned into a hard line. "I'm not scared. You know me better than that."

"Maybe I don't know you at all."

Eddie's face whitened. "Let's drop it, Al."

Al smiled thinly and was silent. The scar on his face was a red thread. Eddie went over to the window and looked out at the gray beach. They were sitting together, two dark figures on the empty sand. Beyond them was the white charge of the breaking waves.

He saw the glow of a cigarette, a tiny stab in the gray expanse, then he drew the curtains together and wiped it all from his sight.

"We're taking the two days," Al said.

Eddie waited.

"And then we cross them up."

Eddie came slowly over to him. "How do you mean?"

"Just let me figure it out. I'm starting to smell an idea."

He reached over for a cigarette, lit it, smoked quietly. The smoke curled away from the dim light of the lamp and into the room shadows.

Al's fingers drummed on his bare knee. "Yeah, I've got an idea. Not all there yet. But it'll come. We're going to sucker them in. And then run like hell."

"Where?"

"There are lots of places, Eddie. Lots of them."

Eddie shook his head grimly. "These guys found us here. They'll find us again."

The fingers stopped drumming. "Why?"

"Because the hundred grand belongs to them. That's why. And as long as it does they'll keep looking till they find it again."

"I said you were scared and I say it again."

"The hell with you," Eddie said bitterly.

"You're crapping out like you always did." His voice rose. "That's why you never made champ."

"Al."

"Any time the going got rough you crapped out. And you want to do it now."

"Al, I'll clip you!"

"Go ahead. But it won't change anything. You're still what you are. Go ahead, Eddie."

Eddie slowly dropped his fists to his sides. He moved over to a chair and sat down heavily. The room was silent again.

Finally Al spoke. "Eddie."

Eddie didn't answer.

"Eddie, what are we crossing each other up for? We started out together. Didn't we, kid? Didn't we?" His voice trailed off into the stillness.

"Eddie," he said again.

Eddie sighed. "All right, Al. I'll play it your way." Then he added, with a twisted smile, "Don't I always?"

Al grinned across at him. Their shadows hung on the wall. "Now you're talking like the Tiger again. The real Tiger."

"Yeah," Eddie said wryly.

Al got up and came over to him. "The trouble with you, kid, is you try and think. And then you get yourself all tangled up. You're an action guy, Eddie. A boy with two fists. Isn't that how it always was?"

Eddie gazed at the grinning face and didn't answer.

"Any time you thought for yourself you landed flat on your back. Because you didn't listen to Uncle Al. That's why. But now you're on his side again. And you're sitting in the lucky corner. The lucky corner."

He patted Eddie on the shoulder. "We got a big round coming up, kid. A real big one."

The glittering look slowly crept back into the hard eyes. The scar began to redden again. His voice became guttural. "I'm getting those guns tomorrow. I'll find a way to get them. They can tail me with an army but I'll get to those guns."

The words tumbled out rapidly, wildly. Eddie kept staring at the glittering eyes.

"Kill us? We'll kill a few of them before we're done. The guns will make us even. Even with them. A hood's got a gun. That's what makes him strong. Huh, Eddie?"

He thrust his face close to Eddie's. "We go in tomorrow afternoon and we split up. You just mosey around. Let the bastards follow you where they want. But stick on the crowded streets and around the crowded places. They'll follow you, but they'll leave you alone. They won't rough you up. I know how they operate. Then meet me back here at night. And I'll have the guns, Eddie."

The words choked in his throat.

Thirteen

Lying in bed unable to sleep, Eddie felt a light touch upon his shoulder. He turned abruptly.

It was Laura.

"Eddie?"

The night was thinning away and he could see the whiteness of her face and the gleam of her eyes.

"Eddie," she said again.

"Laura."

"Al's sleeping. I have to talk to you."

She sat down on the bed beside him, and in the gray

dimness he could see the swelling of. her lip, where Al had struck her. She put her hand to it, as if to cover it from his stare.

"Are you all right?" he asked.

"I'll be okay."

She dropped her hand from her face and rested it gently upon his thick wrist. "Eddie. Eddie, what's going to happen to me?"

"Everything will turn out all right, Laura."

"I'm scared. I'm scared of him. You saw how he was. Who knows what he'll do next!"

He drew his hand away from hers and sat upright. Their voices were low, almost whispers. Outside, the surf had calmed.

"There's nothing to worry about, Laura. He won't touch you any more. I'll make sure of that."

"But I know about the money and the trouble. I know all about it. And he doesn't like that."

She bent over to him, and he saw the clean curve of her breasts. Then the dark stains of blood on the lace edge of the nightgown.

"He'll kill me, Eddie. You don't know him like I do. You never really knew him. He can be terribly cruel. Eddie, what am I going to do?"

"It'll work out."

She shook her head fiercely. "It's a bad deal, Eddie. I can see it coming. Take me out of it. Take me along with you."

"I'm not going anywhere, Laura."

She bent closer to him. He felt a strange mingling of desire and pity for her.

"Eddie, let's get hold of the money and get out of here. Just you and me, Eddie."

He put his hands on her shoulders and held her away from him. "You'd better get back to your room, Laura. Before he wakes up."

"Please, Eddie. Those guys want the money. Let's take it before they do, Eddie. We'll go away. We'll be good together."

He thought of the way her body had moved with his, her moan. His hands relaxed, an instant.

Then he held her away again. "Get back to Al."

"You're hurting me, Eddie."

"I mean to."

"Eddie."

He released his hold on her, watching her get up from the bed. He could see the hard nipples of her round breasts and the lithe curve of her body through the sheerness of the nightgown.

The thin gray light fell across her. The sound of the surf came softly through the room, beating as though it was his own pulse.

Laura leaned close again, the green eyes pleading. "He's sleeping. I tell you, he's sleeping. I know him like a book. He won't get up for hours."

She put her hands to the silk straps of her gown, her fingernails glistening. "I'm charged up, Eddie. Help me relax a little. I don't know where I'm going. This always relaxes me, Eddie. Just for me."

She started to slip the gown from her body. He rose and came to her.

"Laura, get out. Before I hit you like Al did."

She stared at his harsh face. Then she slowly pulled up the gown and went out of the room.

When the door closed silently, he found himself wondering if he really would have hit her.

Fourteen

Will Al be able to get to the guns? He would need about two hours, he had said as he left Eddie. And he would have to lose Ferer's tail guy first.

Eddie walked along, under a high sparkling sky. The clouds were white and piled up. He suddenly thought of them as huge, airy pillows.

He sighed gently.

He walked on again, his huge bulk shadowing the glass of the store windows. He wanted to get away from it all, to lie down and rest his whirling head, just rest it and let the crowding, turbulent fears weave out of him.

It's not going to work out, he said to himself. It's going to end bad. And I don't know what to do about it.

He ambled along, his thick brown hair glinting in the blaze of the sun. His white suit was clean and shining.

I always liked being down here. I was always happy here. I never knew a time I was not happy here.

But this time.

He stopped and turned and he saw the man stop and casually move over to a store window where he stood studying the display, his two hands thrust into his jacket pockets.

Mateo, Eddie said grimly. Mateo, and his bloody knife.

Eddie turned away and began walking again. Till he saw the long white building and the stretch of grass, green and smooth in the sun.

Suddenly he knew that he had been looking for that building. Deep within, he had been searching.

He crossed the street and went up the flight of stone steps, his heart beating rapidly. When he got inside, he looked around eagerly. All he saw was a wide desk with two elderly women behind it, shelves of books and in the center of the room, long shiny tables.

He shrugged disappointedly and went over to one of the tables and sat down. He picked up a book and thumbed through it. And as he did, hopelessness swept through him.

He knew now how much he had wanted to see her. Just to sit and talk to her. Just that would have been enough.

Then he heard her voice.

"I thought you never went into libraries."

The book dropped out of his hands and onto the table. He saw her standing over him.

"Mia."

"Not so loud, Eddie. People are studying here."

"Mia."

She wore a light gray dress, and it seemed to him that it made her eyes darker and more tender. She sat down by him.

"I've been waiting for you, Eddie."

And as she said that, deep in the background of his consciousness a small fear stirred and began to move, like a shadow.

"Have you, Mia?"

She nodded, a gentle smile playing in the luminous eyes.

"I knew you wouldn't disappoint me."

"Did you, Mia?"

"Yes."

The room was deep and cool and silent; the sun slanted through the high windows and made the ends of the table gleam.

"Do you like it here, Eddie?"

"Uh-huh."

"Do you really mean that?"

"Yes."

"I keep thinking about you, Eddie."

"Do you, Mia?"

"Very much."

"I think of you too. But most of the time I don't know I'm doing it."

"That's a strange thing to say."

"I guess it is."

He shrugged and smiled at her. His eyes kept looking at the clear oval face. The dark shining hair that framed it. Then down to the slender wrist and the tapering fingers that rested on his thick hand.

"I mean that you're with me, even when I'm talking and looking at someone else. I didn't realize that until now."

A mischievous smile came into the dark eyes. "Was it my kiss that did it, Eddie?"

"Maybe."

He was smiling now, too. And he forgot Al and Laura, and the money. Most important of all, he forgot the money.

But deep within him, the fear rustled endlessly.

"And if I hadn't kissed you?"

He didn't say anything.

"You'd still be thinking of me?"

"Still."

She laughed low and melodiously. Then she drew her hand away and rose. "I have to go to the stacks for a while. So stay here."

"The stacks?"

"That's where we keep our reserve books."

"Oh."

As he looked at the tender face with its animated smiling features, she seemed very young. Desperately young. He thought of the fifteen-year-old girl who stood in the shadows of the room while he spoke to the widow of Joey Alcan.

"I'll hurry back, Eddie."

It was after she was gone that he saw the figure of Mateo seated at the other end of the room. He had completely forgotten about him. Eddie's face whitened. He reached for the book on the table and opened it.

He sat staring at the blurred words, trying to force his mind away from the thoughts that pressed in upon it.

His lips thinned into a straight hard line. He snapped the book shut and laid it down. He walked steadily down the length of the room till he came to the man.

"You're starting to get under my skin," he said.

The lips in the narrow, angular face parted in a smile. The lean body rested easily in the chair.

"Ferer said two days. Now get off my back."

The lips smiled, showing an even row of small white teeth. But the eyes under the raven black eyebrows smouldered with hatred.

"No sabe, Señor."

"You *sabe* damn well," Eddie said fiercely.

"Español, Señor."

"You know what I'm saying. You know damn well."

"Español."

Eddie's hands closed into fists. He glared down into the taunting face and wanted to smash it. He wanted to let loose the rage and futility that welled through him.

Then he heard Mia's voice beside him.

"Eddie?"

He slowly turned away from the man.

"Eddie, what's wrong?"

"Nothing, Mia."

His hands lay flat against his sides. His face was still grim and little beads of sweat clustered on his forehead.

"Nothing," he repeated.

"What happened?" she asked Mateo.

He spread his hands wide. *"No sabe, Señorita?"*

"Que pasa?"

"Nada, Señorita."

The leathery face was cold and impassive. Then he said again, *"Nada."*

Mia took Eddie's arm. "Come with me." He hesitated. But she said firmly, "Come, Eddie."

When they came into the hall, she turned to him. "What is it, Eddie?"

"Nothing."

"Nada. Nada. Everybody says nada. You looked ready to hit him. Why?"

He stared past her and into the big room. Mateo still sat there, silent and motionless. And immovable.

"Who is that man?"

"I don't know, Mia."

She frowned. Then she said, "Come."

He followed her till they came to a narrow flight of stone steps. Mia paused and smiled at him. "I thought I'd show you the stacks. That's why I came back so quickly."

"Oh."

"Care to see them?"

"Okay."

"Still feel like hitting somebody?"

He didn't answer. They walked down the stone steps, their footsteps sounding sharply.

"Here we are."

They stood before a metal door. Mia opened it and they went inside. The room was large and lined with steel book shelves that rose to the high ceiling. Mia walked down one of the aisles and stopped.

"You look surprised, Eddie."

"Guess I never saw so many books in one room."

"People read."

"Yeah. I guess they do."

"They read to find out things, Eddie. To better themselves."

He touched one of the books. His face was wistful. "Haven't read a book in years. When I was a kid I used to love them."

"What happened?"

He lifted a book and then abruptly put it back into place. "My old man ran off. My mother died. And I was alone with two fists. That's what happened."

"It's never too late to start again," Mia said.

"For me it is."

"Why?"

He shrugged.

"You don't think much of yourself, do you, Eddie?"

"I'm just a worn-out pug, Mia."

"But there's so much more to you, Eddie. So very much more."

He shook his head. "I'm at the end of the road, Mia. There's nothing in me. And there's nothing ahead."

"Maybe you're at the beginning of a new road, Eddie. And there's everything ahead of you."

She was close to him, and he wanted to put his arms about her and hold her to him.

But then she said. "What's wrong, Eddie?"

And he instinctively drew away. "Wrong?"

"Something is terribly wrong with you. What is it?"

"Nothing."

"Nada?"

Deep within him, the fear stirred again.

"Let's drop it, Mia," he said.

"But I don't want to drop it. I want to know, Eddie."

And he heard himself saying, "Don't you already, Mia?"

Her dark eyes widened. "I?"

He didn't say anything.

"What did you mean by that?"

"Let's drop it."

"What?" she insisted.

"Forget it. I don't know what I meant."

"Eddie, you're in great trouble. I can see it in your face. In your actions. I want you to tell me about it."

"I'm in trouble," he said grimly. "And I don't know who to trust any more," he said bitterly.

"Eddie. Eddie, I must go upstairs now. Please stay here. I must speak to you."

"There's nothing to talk about."

"Please, Eddie. Please."

He looked at her pleading face. At the anguished eyes. And the fear started to subside.

"Please."

"All right," he said reluctantly. "I'll wait."

She pressed his hand gratefully and left him. He walked

restlessly up and down the silent room. The room began to stifle him. He wanted to get outside and into the free sunlight again.

Suddenly the metal door swung shut.

"Doran."

Eddie stood rigid against one of the metal shelves. The heavy footsteps sounded through the closed room.

"Doran."

It was Juan's voice.

And Eddie remembered Al's words: Stay in crowded places. They won't rough you up there.

Eddie turned to run. But there was nothing but the blank wall ahead of him. He swung about.

The huge, hulking figure of Juan stood before him. A gun in his hand. Behind him was the baleful face of Mateo.

"All right, punk," said Juan. He handed the gun to Mateo and moved toward Eddie. "So you tried to be a tough guy upstairs?"

Eddie brought his big hands up.

"Keep them down. At your sides. Or you'll get a slug."

Eddie kept his hands raised.

"Keep them down or I'll tell Ferer I had to kill you."

Mateo nodded silently.

"Down," Juan ordered.

Eddie slowly lowered his hands. As he did, Juan struck a jolting blow that landed hard on Eddie's nose. He reeled back. Juan struck again. And again.

One of Eddie's old cuts ripped open, and the blood began to spurt. Juan hit hard in the spleen, and Eddie gasped out as the pain knifed through him.

"Tough guy. I'll show you how tough you are."

The little eyes were set with a cold fury. He slammed his fists into his ribs and Eddie's breath left him.

Slowly, dazedly Eddie dropped to his knees. Juan bent over and pulled him upright against the steel shelves.

"Stand up. You got more coming, punk."

As he raised his arm to strike Eddie again, Mia's scream pierced the room.

Juan let Eddie slip down to the floor.

Just before the blackness closed down on him, Eddie saw,

in a dim, blurry haze, Juan turn to Mia. His lips moved
rapidly.

Then the two killers left the room.

"Do you feel better now, Eddie?"

"I'm all right, Mia."

He leaned against the wash basin for support. They were
in the little utility room that was next to the stacks.

"You're still weak, Eddie," Mia said anxiously.

"I'll be okay the minute I hit air."

He touched the adhesive over his eyes and grinned mirthlessly. "You'd make a good cut man, Mia. A real good one.
Joey teach you that?"

She didn't speak. Her face was white and drawn.

"You came just in time, Mia. Just when the beating was
about over."

"What?"

"The bell was going to ring."

She came close to him, her eyes flashing. "Eddie, what
are you talking about?"

"It was a setup, wasn't it?"

"Eddie."

"I've been in setups before, Mia. I should know one when
I see it."

"I don't know what you're talking about," she said angrily.

"You left me alone, didn't you? And the spot was perfect
for them."

"I work here. I had to go upstairs."

"What did he say to you when he left?"

"He?"

"The big bastard."

"To keep the police out of this, or he'd kill you." He
stared into her clear angry eyes. Then he said bitterly, "Ah,
who the hell knows what to believe any more."

He turned to go. But she moved over and blocked his way.

"Eddie. Eddie, you're in trouble. And you're going to let
me help you. Whether you want to or not."

"Let me alone," he said.

"No." You're all twisted up. You don't know right from
wrong any more. You don't know who's your friend and
who's your enemy. If you want to talk of bastards, then

talk of that manager of yours. I'm sure he's at the bottom of all this."

"Al's my friend, Mia. He's always been my friend. You talk like them. Like them, Mia."

She shook her head furiously, and he saw with a twinge how beautiful she was. How bewilderingly beautiful. And how desperate his hunger was for her.

"Eddie, I want to see you later and straighten this all out. And help you. Promise you'll meet me. Promise that."

"Mia, I . . ."

"Eddie, I have to be at the Seminole Village at six. I go there every Thursday to read to the children. It's part of the library service. Will you meet me there?"

She put her arms tenderly about him.

"Will you, Eddie?"

"I don't know."

But inside he said, Mia, I've got nothing left but my love for you. Nothing but that, Mia. Nothing. Nothing. I saw you and I loved you. Mia. Mia.

"Eddie, please have faith in me. For Joey's sake."

He didn't speak.

"I'm his daughter, Eddie. Can I ever forget the time you came to us with the money? Can I?"

"I'll be there, Mia," he said.

She kissed him and left.

But after she was gone he remembered that at six the acts were over at the Seminole Village, and the crowds were gone. Only the Indians remained. And they turned their heads away from violence, turned them away stoically.

He began to wonder and fear.

Fifteen

Eddie leaned over the wooden railing and watched the Seminole Indian wrestle with the alligator. The day was starting to fade away and the rays of the sun were now low and slanting. Overhead, the sky was beginning to flush with a faint sweep of redness. The fringed leaves of the palmetto trees rustled gently.

He looked at his watch and thought of the coming darkness.

Quarter past six.

And no Mia.

Eddie cursed softly and watched, as if from a great distance, the copper face of the Indian and the long grotesque jaws of the alligator. It was the last show of the day and there were only a few people standing at the railing of the enclosure. Behind were the dingy thatched houses of the little village, and from them came the smell of burning wood and the scent of frying bananas.

A nickel and dime act, Eddie thought. A guy goes and puts his life on the line for nickels and dimes. And what the hell is different between him and me? Didn't I do the same? Sure, it wasn't for nickels and dimes, but the way it all ended up it was nickels and dimes. And guys get killed in the ring just the same as these fellows do. Joey Alcan. Got hit and never stood up again. The way he lay there that's the way they buried him. So what's the difference?

The alligator swung free and lashed his huge tail. The Indian backed away, his small body tight. He moved in again, suddenly lunged, and locked his arms about the alligator, his back muscles rippling against the blue cloth of his workshirt.

The alligator snorted. The primeval sound slowly vanished.

"Do you think he'll win?" the hard metallic voice said.

Eddie turned sharply and looked into the cold face of Mr. Ferer.

A tremor went through Eddie. "What do you want?" he said.

"*Nada.*"

He wore a Panama hat and a dark blue tropical worsted suit. He leaned his tall, whiplike body against the railing and watched the contest. His profile was sharp in the dying light. Beyond him, among the rustling palmetto trees, stood the figures of Mateo and Juan.

A setup, Eddie said bitterly to himself. A setup.

"Doran."

Eddie waited.

"We've lost your friend."

"Al?"

"Al."

Eddie was silent.

"About two hours ago. Where is he?"

"I don't know."

Ferer's nostrils quivered. The thin, bloodless lips hardened. Ferer didn't speak. He took out a pack of cigarettes and silently offered Eddie one. Eddie shook his head. Ferer lit his cigarette and inhaled. The smoke streamed through the thin nostrils and curled away into the glowing air.

Before them, the struggle continued. Little spots of dark sweat showed through the blue of the shirt. The alligator's teeth flashed and snapped shut but the Indian swung clear of them.

There was a smattering of applause.

"An elusive man," Ferer murmured.

"Fast on his feet," Eddie said involuntarily.

Ferer nodded. "A fighter can appreciate that." He rested his long narrow hand upon the railing. "Your friend is also fast on his feet. And with his mind."

Ferer's lips pressed together into a cruel line. "It's quite a mind, isn't it?" He tapped Eddie's sleeve with one of his long fingers. "But in the end it won't help him. Nor you."

"I don't know where he is, or what he's doing," Eddie said. "I left him in downtown Miami, hours ago. What do you want from me?"

"You know what he's doing."

"I tell you I don't."

The alligator was now on its back. The Indian stepped away quickly, stooped and picked up some sparkling sand. Then he knelt and started rubbing the sand up and down over the alligator's long belly.

"Doran."

"Yeah."

"You're lying."

"I don't sit in Al's skull," Eddie said fiercely.

Ferer dropped his cigarette and slowly ground it dead with his heel. His eyes snapped at Eddie, but he didn't speak.

The alligator seemed asleep. The Indian stepped lightly away and looked up at the circle of faces. His dark eyes glowed with triumph, the nostrils of his straight nose quivered.

Ferer took a half dollar from his pocket and tossed it to the Indian. He caught it deftly in his brown hand, then turned to get the other coins that were being thrown down. They flashed and fell in the red sun.

"He won."

The hulking shadow of Juan fell across Eddie. Then the angular one of Mateo. They stood near him, their dark faces cold as bronze.

"You found a hundred thousand dollars," Ferer said. "The money is not what you think it is."

The alligator was back on its feet again. It moved slowly to the little pond and slowly into it, sending ripples over the stagnant water. The Indian was gone from the enclosure.

The little group of spectators filtered away.

Till Eddie was alone.

With them.

"It is not numbers money."

The sky was now a fierce red above them. Their faces had a pink glow. The air was still about them.

"It was given by people to help free their brothers in another country. One that is south of here. The man with the brief case was bringing the money to me. I was to see to it that it got into the right hands."

Ferer paused. And Eddie thought he saw a mocking look come into his eyes and then vanish.

The face became inscrutable. "Do you know how we found you?"

"How?"

"The case. It was seen by one of our men at the airport. Just after you made your call to me. The little golden head. It is the head of Simon Bolivar, the great liberator. We use it as our emblem."

He straightened to his full height.

"We are many, Doran. There is no escape from us."

The sky began to turn dark. The shadows of the three Spaniards bunched together like a huge hawk.

"We are cruel people. In war there is no choice. Others have been just as cruel to us. My wife and daughter were killed before my eyes."

His voice rose. "Do you understand us better now?"

"I don't know where Al is."

"You lie."

Ferer slapped him savagely across the mouth. The sound rang through the stillness, and Eddie felt the knife blade at his back, its point ready to plunge through.

"We'll take you to a beach, Doran. A lonely one."

The darkness came down upon them with the suddenness of a fist.

Sixteen

When they started the fire he broke loose from them and began to hit about him with a maniacal fury. His fists found Juan's fleshy face and pounded into it again and again. His knuckles felt the snap and break of teeth and the warm spill of blood over them.

But then Mateo slammed the barrel of his gun against the back of Eddie's head, and Eddie staggered and fell forward, unconscious.

When he came to, he was lying on the beach, the smell and heat of the fire close to him. He tried to move, but they had tied him down.

He lay spread-eagled on his back. Arms and legs wide apart.

He was stark naked.

A wind ran across the wide beach, spraying up the sand. Some of it got into Eddie's mouth and eyes.

He coughed.

"Doran."

Ferer's visage was ghastly in the firelight. Beyond it were the distorted faces of the others. Distorted by the wild lights and shadows of the fire. They looked like the night figures of one of Goya's dark and powerful paintings.

"Doran."

Eddie turned his head away to the black emptiness of the night. Then he heard Ferer's voice close to him.

"Where is he?"

"I don't know."

"I see," Ferer said curtly.

Mateo came over to Eddie, a piece of driftwood flaring in his hand. He held it close to Eddie's chest. The fire began singeing the hairs.

"Well, Doran?"

Eddie shut his lips tight and gritted his teeth. When the fire hit into his chest it tore open his lips.

"God!"

He groaned again and again. He sought the sweep of the night sky, as if that would cool away his pain.

"What is Walker planning?"

"I don't know," Eddie groaned. "I don't know."

And as he said that a fierce rage welled up in him. At their cruelty to him.

The brand was pressed again to Eddie's skin and he cried out, swinging his head from side to side.

"Doran."

"Ask him. Don't ask me. Find him and ask him."

A bitter smile came to Ferer's lips. "We'll find him. And we'll work him over. But it will gain us nothing. I've dealt with his kind too often."

"I'm the same as him. The same."

"You're not the same."

And this time the fire bit in at the pit of his stomach. And with the searing pain a great fear arose.

"Doran, you fool. We know Walker has the money. We've been watching the bank all afternoon."

The wind blew the sand, the fire sputtered and crackled. The faces and figures wavered.

"He's got the key," Eddie cried out. "The money's in his name. You know all that. Why burn my guts out?"

"His plans," Ferer said relentlessly.

The fire burnt in, this time close to Eddie's groin. He cried out, his voice breaking against the wall of darkness.

"He doesn't want to give back the money. That's all I know. That's all. Goddam you, that's all!"

"Then you'll get him to return it."

"How? How?"

"You're the only one who can."

"I can't."

"You will. One way or another. You'll convince him or

you'll betray him. One way or the other. Is that clear to you?"

He turned his head and nodded curtly. Mateo came over to Eddie and knelt by him. There was the flash of a knife blade. Then Eddie felt the point touch him.

The touch was worse than the searing fire. Because of the terror it brought to Eddie's being.

"You will," Ferer said. "Or you'll stop being a man."

"Ahora," Mateo said. *"Lo hago ahora."*

Ferer shook his head. "I want that money tomorrow morning. Ten o'clock. If it is not there then, we'll come for you."

The knife pressed in.

"And you'll go on the rest of your life wishing every minute of it that you were dead."

The sweat kept running down Eddie's face.

"Ten o'clock, Doran."

They cut the cords.

"The Lorraine."

They left him.

Seventeen

He stood in the small foyer, studying the names on the mail boxes until he saw hers. He put his thick finger to the pearl button that was underneath the name plate and pressed hard. Then he went up the carpeted stairs, his hand gliding along the bronze railing.

When he came to the top of the staircase, he paused and looked along the narrow hall at the closed white doors. Then he saw one open.

"Eddie?"

The door opened wide and she stood on the threshold, gazing at him.

"Hello, Mia," he said grimly.

"Eddie."

"Surprised? Your name's in the phone book. You're easy to find, Mia."

He glanced away from her and down the sweep of steps till he saw the shadows in the foyer.

"Your pals."

"What?"

"Nothing."

He followed her into the apartment and stood watching her close the door. She wore a figured dressing gown of dark green; her dark shining hair was upswept. It made her face look Grecian.

Her simple beauty cut through him.

"Eddie, I'm so glad you came. I've been worried about you. I . . ."

"What happened, Mia?" he cut in.

"I was delayed. I got there at six-thirty and you were gone. Why didn't you wait? Why?"

"I had another appointment," he said.

The room was long and low, with light gray walls; at the end were two narrow louvered windows that made him instantly think of the Lorraine. Beyond the windows was the reach of the night.

He looked at the white pebbled fabric of the furniture, at the long sofa that gleamed under the light of its two flanking lamps. Then at the rest of the room as it dimmed away from the flash of light till the far walls were in complete shadow.

"Looks expensive."

"It is."

She had moved away from him, and was now standing in the shadows. Her eyes looked almost warily at his grim figure.

"Who pays, Mia?"

"I do."

"You got a kitchen and a bedroom. You're in a pretty fancy neighborhood. Who pays, Mia?"

"Eddie, what is this?"

"You tell me."

"I pay for it. Who else? It's more than I can afford, but I love it, and so I pay for it."

She moved out of the shadows to him. Her clear skin glowed in the lamplight.

"On a librarian's salary?"

"Yes."

Her voice rose and her dark eyes flashed. "Eddie, why do you speak to me this way? Why?"

"How do you want me to speak to you, Mia? After what happened."

"I was delayed. I told you that."

"Yeah. On purpose."

"Joey Alcan's daughter. Joey would've killed you for what you did. He's turning over in his grave now."

The color drained from her cheeks. Her lips trembled. He felt a tightening in his heart as he saw the hurt he had given her. But he went on. "You did a job on me, Mia. A swell job."

"Job? What job?" she said in an agonized voice. "Eddie, what have I done that you treat me this way? I know what you're going through, but does it give you the right to . . ."

Her voice choked up and she couldn't go on. He turned away from her and was silent. The silken drapes rustled softly in the night breeze. Then he heard the thin sigh of the palm trees; and they were still again.

"Eddie. Eddie, what have I done?"

He didn't answer.

"Why do you torture me this way?"

He turned back to her and his gray eyes glinted fiercely. "Ferer, Mia. Ferer."

"Ferer?"

"You tell me."

"Tell you what? What?"

"Ferer. The hundred grand. The bank."

She stood there, a frantic, bewildered look on her face. "This, Mia. This!"

His hands tore open his shirt. She gasped when she saw the raw, red flesh, as if he had struck her.

"Eddie!" And her voice was like a scream.

"This. This. They gave me a going over. Your pals gave me a real good one this time. And you set them up, Mia. You."

"I?"

He reached out savagely and gripped her hands. "Mia. Mia, why don't you level with me?"

"Eddie, please. Please."

"You know I got the hundred grand. And you know how Ferer is trying to get it away from me."

"I don't know. I don't."

"But you do," he said hoarsely. "How the hell does he know the money's in the bank? How?"

"You're hurting me."

She tried to twist away from him, but in his fury his grip tightened.

"You're the only one who saw us put it in. You were there when Al came up with the brief case."

He loomed over her. "The brief case, Mia. The brief case. That was the tipoff. All the way down the line."

"Eddie."

Her voice broke and he saw the tears come into her eyes. His fury started to leave him, quicker than it had come. He released his hold on her.

"Eddie, I don't know what you're talking about. All I know is that you're scaring me. For you. For you."

"Yeah. For me."

The tears were now streaming down the oval face. The lips quivered. She turned her head away from him and began to sob. "For you. Can't you see that, Eddie? Can't you?"

He felt a sudden urge to reach out his big hand and touch the smooth, shining hair. Touch it tenderly and with that touch take away the tears. But instead he swung about and went to the windows and stood there, staring out into the night.

When the sobbing had ceased, he spoke to her. Each word was slow and deliberate. "You were with them all the time. The bank. And then the way you found me at the motel. And made me come running after you. Made me fall in love with you."

"Love, Eddie?"

He felt her come close to him.

"Love?"

"You know that better than I do, Mia."

"I only know it now. Now."

He shook his head grimly. "No, Mia. It was there in my big dumb face from the first minute I saw you. I'm an easy guy to read." He added bitterly, "A real easy guy."

The tears were back in her eyes again. She reached her hand out to his but he drew away from her.

"The act is over. Why go on with it?"

"Eddie, you wrong me so. And yourself. Yourself, Eddie. Because I love you too. Can't you see that?"

And she repeated softly, "Love you, too."

"No," he said hoarsely, his face tense and agonized. "No."

"With all my heart."

"No, Mia."

But within he trembled and fought desperately to believe. Because he knew at the core of his being that without belief there was nothing. Nothing left for him.

"I love you, Eddie," she said. "Longer than you have loved me. Longer. Much longer. From the time you came to us with the money in your hand. I loved you then for what you were. A big decent man with a heart as big as his body. And I loved your face, too. The color of your hair and the gray of your eyes. And the way you spoke, in that big yet gentle voice. I loved you then, Eddie. I love you now."

He moved a few steps to her and then he stopped.

"Eddie," she said. "Can't you believe me? Why do you fight away from me? I know nothing about this Ferer or the money. Nothing."

He stood there, his body aching to feel her nearness. She came closer.

"Why do you come to me with such twisted thoughts, Eddie? Why didn't you come to me and say, 'I'm hurt. Help me, Mia. I'm hurt.' But instead you come as you would to an enemy. An enemy."

She touched his cheek and kissed it, sending a throb through him. She whispered, "Believe in me, Eddie. Believe."

"Mia. Mia."

Her hair brushed close to his face and then strayed over his lips. Her delicate scent was all about him.

"Please. Please."

All about him, making his blood pound and causing the words to rush to his tight lips, and then break through them.

"Mia. I want so much to believe you. I never loved anybody before. Never in the years I knocked around. There were always girls but never anybody I loved. Not till you came into my life. Not till then."

"If you love me then you believe me."

She pressed closer to him, her eyes pleading, her cheeks flushed and hot. The dark green dressing gown had fallen open and he felt the softness of her breasts against the seared flesh of his body. Soft and yielding and cooling. While in his head a hammering began.

"Mia."

"If you love me as I love you," she whispered.

Her lips were upon his. Her body quivered in his arms. Her legs trembled against his.

"Mia."

"Eddie. Hold me closer, dearest. Dearest. Dearest."

He kissed her again and again and as he did he saw Mateo's face in the flickering firelight. The poised knife. Its blade hot to his flesh. And for a fleeting instant his body stiffened with terror. Then the instant passed and he began to love Mia with a harsh and desperate hunger.

And as he did, all his doubts and fears vanished.

Only Mia naked in his arms remained.

Only Mia.

Mia.

Eighteen

He opened the door and stepped into his room. He was about to snap on the light when he heard Al's voice.

"Keep it off, Eddie."

Then he saw the solid figure seated on the white bed. The curtains were drawn together and the room was dark. The light from the corridor crept in under the door in a thin line.

Eddie went over to the bed.

"I've been waiting for you," Al said.

"I'm here."

"Good." Al's face appeared harsh and grim in the flare of a match and then vanished back into the darkness. The smell of cigarette smoke weaved about the room. "You've been followed much?" he asked.

"I've been followed."

"Sons of bitches were on my back like monkeys. Wouldn't let go for a minute." He laughed low and then said, "But I was able to throw them. For a good two hours."

He grunted. "When they picked up my trail again, they let me have it. Cut me off at a road crossing. Just about sundown. They beat the crap outa me. Looking for the guns."

"They find them?"

"Had them hidden under the car. Tied to the muffler. No, Eddie. They didn't find them."

"Al?"

"Yeah?"

"Ferer wants the money."

No sound came from the beach; the ocean was wide and silent.

"And?"

"Tomorrow. At ten."

The cigarette glowed in the darkness.

"We're to bring it to the Lorraine. Or else."

"Or else my can," Al said. "The hell with him." Eddie sighed low and then said, "I've been thinking it over, Al. Doing some real hard thinking. From all angles."

"And?"

Eddie paused and then said, "I want you to give the money over to him."

"What?"

"It's on my back. I want it off once and for all."

He heard the creak of the bed as Al's body swung off it. Then he saw the solid figure come through the darkness and over to him. The face was in shadows, but the eyes stood out fierce and bright.

"What's with you, Eddie? What?"

"I told you I've been doing some thinking."

Al's voice rang through the room. "The hell with your thinking," he said. "The hell with it. I told you to leave that to me. Goddam you, Eddie, I told you that."

His hand reached out and grabbed Eddie's shoulder. "Where the hell have you been that you come up with such talk now? Where, Eddie?"

"Take your hand off, Al."

"Where? I got everything all set up. We're ready to sucker

the bastards and take off and you come up with this. With this!"

"Take your goddam hand off me."

Al slowly released his grip. His breath came in short heavy gasps. "Where were you, Eddie?"

"Where?" Eddie suddenly burst out. "On a beach bare-ass while Ferer tried to burn my guts out."

"What do you mean?"

"They gave me the works because you ducked out on them."

"The Spic sons of bitches."

"They had a knife at my nuts. Ready to cut them off." His voice rose. "They want the money, Al!"

"Numbers guys. That's how numbers guys operate. Especially the Spic ones. They go right for where you live. Real savages."

"They're not numbers at all. The money was collected for some revolution in South America."

"What?"

"South America somewhere."

"South America," Al said with a short hard laugh. "Who told you that? Ferer?"

Eddie was silent.

"Ferer. He tries all ways on you, don't he, Eddie? He'll burn you and soft-soap you all at the same time. He's a real cutie, isn't he?"

"Stop laughing at me, Al."

"Revolution. South America."

His mocking laughter filled the room. Eddie rose swiftly and faced him. His hands closed into big fists.

"Stop laughing, Al, or I'll clip you."

The laughter died out. Then Al said, "I wasn't laughing at you, Eddie. If anybody's doing any laughing, they are."

He turned away from him and went over to the bed and sat down. Eddie stood still in the darkness, his face tense and white. Then he heard the manager's voice.

"Revolution. What a load of crap this Ferer baby can sling. Especially when he's up against a big simple joker like you."

Eddie moved forward a step. "Take it easy, Al. Stop crowding me."

"I'll crowd you to hell and back when it comes to a

hundred grand. Revolution. South America. What else did he tell you? That his belly's all wrapped up in a Spanish flag? I suppose he gave you a song and dance about starving people. Starving people and a dictator snapping the whip over them. And you taking the money away from these poor people. Eddie Doran, the big louse."

"Shut up!"

But the voice went grimly on. "Your heart's always in your face, Eddie. And this guy Ferer plays both sides of the street with you. If he can't burn the money out of you, he'll soft-talk it out. Why didn't he try that load of crap with me?"

Eddie was silent.

Al laughed in a low, taunting voice. "Because he knows I'd spit it right back into his eye. They're numbers, Eddie. Tough and hard. And for a hundred grand I can be just as tough and hard."

His voice rose. "Yeah, even tougher. I picked up the guns, Eddie. And now they can go hump themselves for all I care. And if you want to drop out now that's okay with me."

"What?"

"That's what I said, Eddie. I didn't screw you up to now. I kept my part of the bargain. It was to be an even split down the line. That's how we always operated, wasn't it?"

Even from across the room Eddie could still see the glitter in the black eyes.

"If the money's on your back, fine. Just shift it all over to mine. I can carry it. All the way, Eddie."

And he thought he could see the scar, threading down the dark face.

"I'll take them on alone, Eddie. I got nothing to lose and everything to gain. And if they get me, okay. At least I'll know I went down with a hundred grand in my hands."

Eddie listened to the voice and thought of Mia and how much he wanted to be free of the money.

Mia in his arms, and the world was full of hope again. He was no longer a cast-off pug with nowhere to go, but a man in love, a man who had everywhere to go.

"You know where I got this scar, Eddie? When I was a kid, before I met up with you, a guy tried to take something from me. Something that was mine. He ripped my face open, but I still held on to what I had. Yeah, the blood was coming down all over me, but I held on. He never got it, Eddie. Never."

But the money, the hated money, still stood between them. Until it was back to where it belonged, there would never be any peace in his soul.

"So if you want me to take over, just let me know. I'll walk out of this room and you'll never see me again."

"Al," Eddie suddenly shouted. "The hell with the money! The hell with it! The hell with it! So it's numbers money, the hell with it! Let them have it and let them screw themselves with it. Give it back. I want you to get it and give it back. It's starting to stink!"

"No."

He moved swiftly over to the bed, his face taut. "It's got to go back. Do you hear me?"

"I said, no."

"Al!"

He reached his big hands out to grab him, but as he did he saw the glint of the gun barrel.

"Stay put, Eddie."

"Al."

"Stay put or I'll kill you."

Eddie stood there, his hands tense at his sides. The barrel was pointed straight at his head. Al's face was like a block of stone, gray in the darkness.

Then he heard him say, "Listen, you damn fool. Listen to me. You're being taken for a ride. All the way. Even Joey Alcan's daughter is in on it."

"Mia?"

"Mia Alvarez. She's in with them, you jerk. I told you not to trust her. I told you the minute I saw her."

Eddie's hands trembled. And he felt the sweat break out upon his cold forehead.

"She was out to see you on the beach, wasn't she? I know she was. Laura saw her with you. Saw her kissing you. Was that where you were tonight? Is that where you got the big ideas?"

"Mia?" Eddie whispered.

"In with them. Part of the Ferer deal."

"Not Mia."

"Yes. She wants you to give the money back, doesn't she?"

Eddie looked silently down at the harsh face. And as he looked he felt the whirling, lost feeling begin within. As if it had never ended, but was always lying there, always, always.

He heard Al's voice as if it came from a great distance.

"It's the old confidence gimmick. The girl. Use the girl. You get more with a pair of legs, more and quicker than you'll ever get with a gun. She knows how to use those legs, doesn't she, Eddie?"

And Eddie heard himself shout, "Shut up, Al! I'll kill you, gun or no gun!"

"Okay, Eddie."

The room was silent again. Eddie turned slowly away from him and went over to the window and stood there. Then his hands opened the curtains a bit and he stared into the black night, searching for the cooling sight of the ocean.

Somehow he felt that if he could see it, see it flashing, the pain would leave him.

But all he saw was the dark sweep of the night. Then after a while he said in a dull voice, "How did you know?"

"After I picked up the guns I went back to Collins Avenue. I saw her talking to one of the guys who had been tailing me."

Eddie didn't say anything.

"They were standing in front of the bank, Eddie."

"Ferer knows the money is in the bank," Eddie said, almost to himself.

"And how do you think he knows?"

Al's voice clipped out again. "How?"

Eddie's eyes kept thrusting into the night, the big head bent forward tautly. The image of Mia rose up before him. Mia standing in the splash of sunlight, her black hair shining and the eyes looking luminously into his.

"They're numbers, Eddie. She's with them."

The night rushed in and blotted out Mia's shining figure. The luminous eyes vanished and all that remained was emptiness.

Eddie fiercely drew the curtains together again. His hands dropped slackly to his sides.

The destroying voice began again. "They got you coming and going, Eddie. If they can't burn it out of you they'll screw it out of you. Coming and going. What do you really know about her? What, Eddie?"

"Nothing," Eddie said.

"Nothing but that she's Joey Alcan's daughter. And that's it. Suddenly she comes out of nowhere and right into your life. From out of nowhere, Eddie. You've been doing a lot of thinking. Well, think on that one a while. Did you ever know that Joey Alcan was mixed up with some Spic hoods? Did you?"

"No."

"Well, he was. And he threw two fights for them. They made their dough and then they dumped him."

"Joey was not the kind to go into a tank."

"I'm telling you he did. Twice. They dumped him because he was no longer of any use to them. But he was marked all right in their book. And I'm betting you a thousand to one this Ferer guy is of the same mob. That's how your girl friend comes to be with them."

Eddie went away from the window and over to the chair. He sat down slowly and heavily upon it. His hands dangled.

"These Spics stick together, Eddie. They were always that way. You should know that."

"I don't know anything any more."

"Still feel like giving the money back?"

The bed creaked and Al got up and came over to him. Eddie saw the light threading along the gun barrel.

"It's yours, Eddie."

Then he felt the grim weight of the gun as Al dropped it into his jacket pocket.

"Keep it, pal. I got one, too. Nobody's going to get you on any beach any more bare-ass. Nobody's going to horse you around. Not with that in your fist, Eddie. Not with that!"

Eddie's fingers touched the cold metal and then drew away.

"We're back in business, Tiger. Aren't we?"

"Who the hell knows?" Eddie muttered.

"We're back in business and tomorrow we'll pick up the money and get the hell out of here."

Eddie felt the manager's hand go to his head and rub it vigorously. "Forget her. It was a bad deal and it's over now."

Eddie jerked his head away.

"You're starting to get angry, Eddie. And that's a good sign. A real good sign."

Eddie looked up at the patch of face and said harshly, "You got some drinks in your room?"

"Sure, Eddie boy," Al said.

"I could use a few."

"Sure, Eddie. Just killed a bottle with Laura, but there's always more left. Liquor we always got enough, huh kid?"

Eddie saw him go to the door. Just as the hand reached for the glimmering knob, Eddie asked, "What about Laura?"

Al stopped and turned. "What do you mean?"

"How does she figure in on tomorrow?"

"She's in, Eddie. All the way."

He came back through the gloom to him. "I'm making it up to her for the way I treated her last night."

"You should," Eddie grunted.

"I was off balance. You know I'm not that way with her. I got thrown. You never saw me hit her before, did you? Did you?"

"No."

"I was the guy who made you take her down here, wasn't I? And then I got to go and clout her. Off balance, Eddie."

"You were."

"But I'm back in saddle with her. Just had one of the greatest times with her. The greatest."

"Get the drinks," Eddie said.

"Coming up, Tiger."

The door opened and closed. Eddie was alone in the darkness.

Nineteen

He had told Mia that he was going to return the money to Ferer. Once and for all he was going to face up to Al, make him get the money out of the vault box and hand it over. Once and for all. Then he would drive to the Lorraine and rid himself of the hated hundred grand. After that he would call Mia and tell her he was free of it.

He had told Mia that when he was in her arms, the tender darkness hovering about them.

Now it was sunlight, harsh and glaring sunlight. Now he sat in the open car, Laura and Al on either side of him.

"Looks like it's going to be a good day," Al said.

"Yeah."

"A real good one, Tiger. Huh?"

"We'll make it."

"That's the spirit."

Laura sat silent, her tanned arm leaning on the door, her hair glinting red in the sun. The small face was taut.

"How do you feel, Laura?" Al asked.

"Fine."

"You know what to do?"

"I know what to do."

"Check."

His thick hand rested lightly on the steering wheel; a sardonic smile played on his lips. Eddie glanced at him and then away.

Looking at Al's face, he had felt a sudden sense of unreality sweep through him. They were not on their way to a bank but just driving along under a tropical sun—three people out for a joy ride.

But his hand went to his pocket and felt the cold metal of the gun, and he knew that everything was real.

"You didn't have much for breakfast, Laura," Al said.

"Didn't have much of an appetite."

He chuckled. Then he said, "Don't let it get you, baby."

"I won't."

Al had gone over the plan step by step with them. He had wakened Laura and brought her into the room with him. They had sat in the darkness, drinking and talking. Eddie remembered how coldly and precisely the manager had spoken, while outside on the beach somewhere in the night, the two figures stood motionless.

The same two figures sat now in a car following them.

"I feel like having a swim," Al said, staring at the sparkling sky. "It's a shame we don't have time for it."

Then he added with a grim smile. "But we'll have time later on, eh Eddie?"

"Yeah."

Al stopped the car for a light and turned and hit him gently on the chest with the back of his hand.

"Cheer up, big guy. This is just like another fight. You're going to win this one."

"We'll win."

"Sure we will. Uncle Al is in your corner."

He glanced back and then chuckled. "Those two guys sure look sweet. I'd like to see their faces when we're through with them. Huh, Eddie?"

"The light's changed," Laura said.

Al winked and nodded. "You're on the ball, Laura."

"Thanks."

He laughed and stepped on the accelerator. The car sped away from the light and down Collins Avenue, the wind ruffling their hair. Overhead the sky was blue and placid.

Eddie suddenly thought of snow, and of the way it had fallen on that gray morning in New York. The morning that he had sat in the kitchen with Al, the brief case flat on the table. The two whisky glasses flanking it like little soldiers.

Two soldiers. He thought of the two men who sat in the car behind them.

"Fate," he said in a low, dull voice.

"What's that, Tiger?"

"Nothing, Al. Nothing."

"Thought I heard you say something."

Eddie shrugged and stared ahead of him at the growing traffic. They were getting close to Lincoln Road. Al stopped for another light. The noise of traffic surrounded them.

"The satchel okay?" he asked.

Eddie touched the blue canvas satchel that rested at his feet. "Yeah, Al."

"It's empty now. Soon it's going to be full. You thinking about that, Tiger?"

"I'm thinking," Eddie said.

Al lit a cigarette and inhaled. The smoke thinned away into the sparkling air. He drove on again, the cigarette held lightly between his glistening lips. The scar on his face showed red in the sun.

The tan roadster kept steadily behind them, the two figures sitting straight and almost motionless.

Like two soldiers, Eddie thought.

"All right," Al suddenly said, and now his voice was low and somber. "We're starting to get close. Laura, you know what to do."

Laura stiffened a bit, then said slowly, "I know."

"Don't slip up now."

Her eyes flashed at him. "I said I know."

"Good."

He flipped the cigarette into the street, and let his hand close over the wheel.

"Eddie, you come in with me. Right?"

Eddie nodded, and as he did, he felt a tightening in the pit of his stomach.

"We're here," Al said.

He drove slowly to the curb and stopped the car. He got out and stood on the sidewalk waiting for Eddie. Eddie reached for the satchel, smiled at Laura's taut, white face, then got out and stood close to the manager.

The tan roadster came up and stopped. The two men warily studied them. Their eyes were black and hard. They both wore white suits; their hair was dark, their faces swarthy and set.

Like twins, Eddie thought. Only one guy is older than the other. Much older. His face looks like it was through a fire. Scorched and scarred.

"Let's go," Al said.

Eddie followed the stocky manager into the bank. He glanced back into the sweep of sunlight and saw the two men still seated in their car.

"Wait here, Eddie."

Eddie nodded and handed the satchel over. Then he watched Al go down the flight of stone steps and disappear into the gloom below. The bank floor was cool and quiet. There were few people around. Eddie examined each person, until his gaze stopped dead.

Mateo was leaning on one of the counters, his hand resting casually in his jacket pocket. The leathery face was drawn.

"Okay, you bastard," Eddie muttered. "So you're here too."

Then he saw Juan come out of the sunshine and into the shade of the bank. The huge man went over to Mateo and stood by him.

Eddie turned and looked down the flight of steps, while a cold sweat started to break out all over him. From the street came the murmur of the morning traffic and the sounds of people passing.

Within the vaulted room of the bank, all seemed hushed and expectant to Eddie. His eyes kept searching the empty steps. His hand went to his pocket and closed over the cold gun.

He kept his hand on the gun, gripping it tightly to stop his trembling. His palm and fingers were wet. Out of the corner of his eyes he saw the bank guard approaching.

Eddie took his hand out of his pocket and raised it to his head, letting it run over his hair. He took a handkerchief out of his pants pocket and wiped his brow.

The bank guard moved away.

"What the hell's keeping Al?" he muttered. "What the hell's keeping him so long?"

He gazed down the flight of stone steps, his eyes straining to see through the gloom and into the harsh light of the vault room. His body stood tense and quivering.

It was then that he heard her voice.

"Eddie."

He turned sharply and saw her standing before him. The dark, luminous eyes pleading desperately.

"Mia." The word broke out from him, low and agonized.

"Eddie. Eddie, don't do it. You're going back on your word. I can see that you are. Eddie."

He stared at the oval face, its skin now blanched. She reached her hand to his and touched it. A throb of pain spun through him.

"Eddie. Why? Why?"

He looked past her to the figures at the counter, and he said in a low toneless voice, "You're with them."

"No, Eddie."

"Yes. Yes. Why did you lie to me last night, Mia? Why?"

"But I didn't."

"Why, Mia?"

"Eddie, I love you and I ask you to believe in me."

He shook his head grimly at her. "It's too late for that, Mia."

"Eddie, don't try anything. I beg you. Please do as we agreed. I beg you."

"Is that why you're here, Mia? Because Ferer ordered

you? How much are you getting paid? What's your cut of the hundred grand?"

He saw the tears start in her eyes, but he went on bitterly, "How much, Mia?"

"Eddie, I'm paid nothing. Nothing. I came here with hope, with joy, and now you. . . ."

"Yeah," he cut in bitterly. "I know the whole pitch. Save it. It won't cut ice with me any more."

She shook her head desperately. "Eddie . . ."

Her voice choked up and she couldn't go on. He wanted to reach out and take her in his arms, but instead he heard himself saying savagely, "You took me for a ride, Mia. And the ride's over."

"No. No."

But before he could speak again he heard Al's crisp voice behind him.

"Let's go."

He turned from her and saw the satchel gripped in Al's hand. No longer empty.

Eddie nodded curtly. "Okay."

"You'd better stay clear, sister," Al said to Mia. She put her hand on Eddie's arm and stood in his way. "Eddie, don't do it."

"It's done, Mia," Eddie said.

He put her gently aside and started walking to the entrance with Al. All the time he sensed her behind him, her eyes frantically following him.

The bank guard came over quickly and stopped them, just as they were about to go out. "Just a minute, please."

"What's wrong?" Al said.

The guard glanced back to Mia and then to them. "That's what I'd like to know."

"Look," Al said. "I had some money and valuables in a vault box. I just took them out. Anything wrong with that?"

"No," the guard said slowly.

"The dame was bothering us. You mind if we go now?"

"It's my job to ask questions. When I think they should be asked."

"You've asked them."

Eddie looked back at Mia. Then he saw Mateo move away from the counter and go over to her.

"You've asked them," Al repeated, his voice getting tight.

"I'm sorry if I troubled you," the guard said.

He moved out of their way and they went outside the bank and onto the sun-swept sidewalk.

"The guard did us good," Al said. "The jokers in there saw him talking to us, so they kept away. I didn't want them too close to us when we got outside."

Laura sat at the wheel of the car, watching them. When Al nodded slightly, she swung the car out into the line of traffic.

"Come on, Eddie."

"Okay."

They started walking down the busy block. The two men got out of the tan roadster and began following them. Al quickened the pace, threading his way through the people, Eddie at his back.

"The tickets I picked up yesterday."

"Okay, Al."

"Be ready with 'em. It's going to give us the jump we need. Move faster."

They crossed the street against the light and hurried till they came to the theater. Then they turned sharply and went in under the marquee.

"Move your ass, Eddie. Every second counts!"

They moved rapidly past the cashier's window and into the lobby to the ticket taker. Eddie handed the tickets over and they went inside into the darkness.

The orchestra was empty at that hour. There were only a few shadowy heads.

"Up here."

They ran up the dim-lit steps to the balcony. The building had a hollow, cavernous feel to it. The voices from the screen echoed against the walls.

"Quick."

They crossed over to the red light that hung over the exit door. It threw its lurid rays down upon them.

"Okay so far," Al panted. He pushed hard against the door and it swung open, bringing in a shaft of daylight. They went out onto the iron fire escape and looked down into an empty alley. The blind wall of an office building and that of the theater loomed up about them.

Al closed the door partly, letting only a sliver of light filter into the theater.

"Bait."

Then he and Eddie leaned against the railing of the fire escape and waited.

"They're searching the orchestra now," Al said.

"They'll be coming up soon."

"Uh-huh."

"They'll see the door open and they'll know we beat it out this way."

"That's the plan, Tiger."

Al pointed ahead of him. There, between the break of the two walls, Eddie could see the sunlight falling on the small parking lot that belonged to the theater. There were no cars in it.

Beyond the parking lot, across a narrow side street, was a grove of orange trees. At its far end stood an old wooden building which had been Capirani Restaurant. It was now closed and out of use.

"After we take care of these jokers we go through the lot. Then cross the street and into the grove. Got it?"

Eddie nodded.

"Laura will be waiting for us in the Capirani driveway."

"What if she's tailed?"

"Sure she'll be tailed. That's step two. But first we take care of this. Quiet. I can smell the bastards."

They tensed and waited.

"Now," Al whispered.

A drop of sweat trickled down his lean jaw and fell.

The door suddenly opened and they came out with a rush. Al hit the first one a smashing blow on the side of the head. The hard butt of his gun struck again. The man spun, then toppled back and down the iron steps, his body making a crunching sound, till it lay still at the bottom.

Eddie leaned against the door, slamming it shut, then hit hard with his fists. The man with the scorched face let out a cry and staggered back. There was a flash of fire. The bark of a gun. A bullet ripped through Eddie's sleeve, grazing his arm.

He lashed out again, knocking the gun out of the hand of the staggering man. Jamming his fist into the scarred face, he heard the sickening sound of the jawbone as it broke.

The man slid down before him.

Eddie stood staring at him. Till he heard Al's voice from below.

"Come on, you big bastard. Come on!"

He ran down the steps of the fire escape, making them ring. Then he stepped across the fallen body at the bottom and rushed across the lot.

They sped over the silent side street and plunged into the orange grove. As they went through the trees, Eddie remembered, with a pang, the old restaurant and the white-haired man who ran it. And how he loved and tended those trees.

Eddie saw a lone wrinkled orange on one of the trees and he wanted to pause and put his hand to the glowing, forlorn fruit.

"Eddie."

Al had stopped ahead of him. Through a break in the trees they could see the dilapidated building. Then the glint of Laura's hair as she sat in the car. The car was parked in the gravel roadway, it's motor running.

"Keep still," Al whispered. "They're around here."

Eddie crouched, his body tense. He gripped the satchel in one hand, the gun in the other.

"Wait here," Al whispered. "Maybe I can get behind them."

Eddie watched him move off and disappear behind the leaves. All was still. Only the sound of the car motor remained.

Like the heavy breathing of a feral animal.

Ready to pounce.

Suddenly Eddie swung around. But it was too late. A gun barrel smashed into his face. He reeled backwards. Another slashing blow and he dropped to his knees.

Juan threw his huge bulk forward and clubbed Eddie again. Eddie sprawled on the ground.

Then he felt the muzzle of Juan's gun against his head. "I promised you this," Juan said.

Eddie heard the cylinders click. He lay there, senses swirling, waiting for the bullet.

Each split second was a frozen eternity.

Then, as though from a great distance he heard a shot.

The muzzle dropped away from Eddie's head.

Juan stiffened, then toppled to the ground, like a stone man. A gaping hole in his forehead.

"Eddie. Eddie."

Eddie looked up into Al's tense face.

"Get up, you bastard. Come on."

He got to his feet and followed Al through the trees.

"The other Spic is nowhere around," Al said.

Al stopped suddenly and held him back. They were at the fringe of the trees. The car stood in the open before them. They could see Laura's eyes, wild with fright.

"I can't figure out where the other bastard is," Al whispered.

"Maybe he beat it."

"Maybe not."

"We'd better get the hell out of here fast."

"Don't I know that?"

Al still held him back. He searched about frantically, his eyes trying to pierce the foliage of the trees. Then he said desperately, "We can't stay here any longer. Run for the car."

They rushed into the open and were about to reach the car when they heard the sharp voice.

"Stay. You stay."

Mateo came from the back side of the building. His gun pointed at them.

Eddie saw Al about to raise his hand and he said quickly, "No use, Al. You haven't a chance."

Al dropped his gun to the ground. Eddie's was back among the trees.

"Sonofabitch," Al said in a low, toneless voice. "Sonofabitch."

"Stay," Mateo repeated.

He pointed to the bag in Eddie's hand. He began to approach, slowly.

It's all over, Eddie said to himself.

Mateo kept coming, his dark eyes fixed on the bag, the gun held sharply on them.

As he crossed in front of the car to get to them the motor suddenly roared like a wild beast.

He screamed once as the car hit him, pinning him against the wall of the house.

Laura backed the car away from the crushed, lifeless figure. Eddie and Al stood still as statues. Then Al stirred himself. "Come on."

Eddie didn't move.

Al hit him sharply across his face. "Eddie!" He pulled

Al hit him sharply across his face. "Eddie!" He pulled Eddie to the car. Pushing Laura over. Al got into the driver's seat. Laura's eyes had a dead, glassy look.

The car backed out of the driveway and roared away. Al reached down and patted the bag.

"We got the money," he said.

"We got the money," Eddie said.

No one spoke again.

When they hit the highway, they swung south and headed for the Keys.

Twenty

When they got to Key Largo, Al swung the car off the highway and down a narrow, isolated road that led to the Gulf. The sky had blackened, and now the rain began to come down hard.

"This is good," Al said. "It's going to help us."

The rain slashed at the car. The trees around them swayed in the wind. Al put the lights on.

"This is the end of the world," he said. "No one ever goes here. We'll be okay."

Laura sat hunched between them, her green eyes staring ahead into the wall of rain. Her face was pale, her lips partly open. No one had spoken much during the past hours. Each seemed centered in his own thoughts.

All around them, hemming them in, was a thickness of trees and wild growth. The muddy road cut its way through, winding and turning, till it ended abruptly.

They saw the lashing waters of the Gulf directly in front of them. Al drove the car along the water's edge a short distance, then brought it to a halt.

"Last stop. All out."

Ahead of them loomed a paint-peeled, clapboard house, its wet roof sagging. The glass of the broken windows gleamed hollowly.

"Used to belong to a fisherman I once knew," Al said. "He used to fish for whisky in Prohibition days."

"Looks pretty beat," Laura said.

"Couldn't buy it for a million dollars. It's just what we need to hole up in. We'll stay here till it's dark and then go on to Marathon. I'll pick up a boat there and then I'll show you a little island that nobody but God and me knows about."

He chuckled and patted Eddie on the arm. "Uncle Al taking care of you all right?"

Eddie nodded.

"Give me the satchel, Eddie."

"The satchel?"

"Uh-huh."

"Why?"

"I'll hold it from now on in."

They were standing in the driving rain, just outside the house. A clap of thunder shook the sky. Eddie waited till it subsided. Then he repeated, "Why, Al?"

"Because you wouldn't be holding it if it wasn't for me."

Laura stood silently watching them. Her wet hair straggled down over her small face. Her dress clung to her body.

"You getting some ideas, Al?" Eddie said.

"It's still fifty-fifty. But I'd like to hold it." The glitter was back in Al's eyes.

"The money's in your blood," Eddie said.

"You mean there's blood on the money." The rain ran down Al's lean jaw. "Give it over, Eddie."

"Let's get inside," Laura said. "I'm soaked and it's cold out here."

"Take a bottle out of the car. You'll get warm quick enough," Al said. His eyes were fixed on Eddie.

"Let's go in," Laura said, and there was fear in her voice.

"Take a bottle," Al snapped, and he turned fiercely to her.

Laura shrank away from him.

"Easy with her," Eddie warned. "She's been through a lot today. We all have."

"I'm easy," Al said.

He watched her hurry back to the car. She slipped in the mud and almost fell, then got her balance again. Al suddenly laughed, a low, broken laugh. The rain ran down over his face, over the glittering eyes.

The thunder slammed against the sky.

"Well, Eddie?"

"It's in your blood," Eddie said. "Starting to break you apart."

"Eddie! I want it, Eddie!"

"You feel better holding the satchel, okay with me," Eddie finally said.

Eddie handed it over to him. Al grabbed it with a hungry, ferocious gesture. Like an animal springing on prey. "I feel better already," he said.

They killed a bottle among them. But there was no gaiety, no warmth. Al sat by himself, the bag in his hand.

We've gotten away from Ferer, Eddie thought to himself. For a while we're in the clear.

But have we gotten away from ourselves?

They left the house and drove on through the stormy night to Marathon. There they got the boat.

They went through the wind and the rain and the blackness, till they found the little island that only God and Al knew about.

Twenty-One

It's going to end bad, Eddie said to himself.

It's going to end in blood. Soon.

I can feel it coming.

The full moon lit the night like an outsized street lamp. Eddie sat against the trunk of one of the palm trees that dotted the tiny island, and he looked out into the vast and star-swept night. The ocean was quiet and bright with light. Its waters lapped at the rim of the narrow sandy beach with an insistent rhythm.

Behind him, set back among the trees, was the deserted shack they had taken over. Its former occupant had long since gone, leaving behind some old, now rusted, utensils.

The light of the shack gleamed through the trees like a tiny, wavering star.

The night was hot and close, without a stir of air. The

leafy fans of the trees hung motionless and pale. Eddie slapped at a mosquito, and the sound cracked through the silence like a shot.

Then all was still again.

"He's still drinking," Laura said, coming toward him.

"You're drinking too," he said quietly.

"So?"

"So nothing."

She sat down on the sand beside him, her dress pulling up over her knees. Flashes of heat lightning suddenly flared out in the sky and then vanished.

"We just had a time."

"I'm not interested."

"Just telling you."

"You're drunk, or you wouldn't be telling me."

"So I'm drunk."

She played with the sand, scooping it up in her small hand and letting it sift through her fingers to fall in a little sparkling shower. He glanced at her face with its somber eyes and pouting lips. Her mass of hair shone in the moonlight.

"He never takes his eyes off the satchel. Even when he was holding me I knew his eyes were on the satchel."

"And your eyes, Laura?"

She laughed harshly and flung the sand down. "I look but he's got it. That's a big difference, Eddie."

"Yeah, I guess it is."

Her face twisted bitterly. She kicked with her bare foot at the sand. A tiny stream of perspiration trickled down her cheek.

"He talks of Rio. Says we're going to meet up with a boat off Key West and that'll take us down. How the hell are we going to get in to Rio?"

"He's got friends. Al's got friends all over."

"You mean for himself."

She leaned over and he saw that she was wearing nothing but the thin dress.

"For himself, Eddie. All the plans are for himself."

"I don't give a damn one way or another," Eddie said.

"You're a fool. It was you who found the money and it's going to end up all in his lap."

He pushed her back from him. "Then I'm a fool."

"You don't have to be rough with me."

"Just don't lean all over me."

"You didn't say that back at the motel, did you? Then I didn't lean close enough for you."

He started to get up. She put her hand to his knee, the defiant look gone.

"Eddie, don't get sore at me."

"I'm not sore at you, Laura." He sat down again. "Too much to drink. It's starting to throw me."

She let her moist hand rest on his knee, and this time he didn't move away. "He'll give me a few hundred bucks and then kick me out."

Eddie looked away toward the arc of the sky. He saw the jagged flare of the heat lightning again. It throbbed through him.

"I don't know what he's got in mind, Laura. All I know is that he wants to get the hell out of the country. And he thinks that once he's out, the hoods will let up."

He shook his head. "They'll follow us clear into hell. This guy Ferer will never let up. Never, Laura."

"You still think of her," Laura said suddenly.

He didn't say anything. Laura bent over close to him, and this time he could see the full roundness of her breasts and the outlines of the dark nipples.

"You're in love with her, Eddie."

The words and her body suddenly overwhelmed him. He grabbed her to him and kissed her hard on the lips. "I'm in love with nobody."

She clung fiercely to him, her nails cutting into his back. "Take me with you, Eddie."

His hand went to the hem of her dress.

"We'll make a great team, Eddie. A great team."

"Sure, Laura."

His fingers touched beneath, and her nails dug deeper into his flesh. "I'll find a way to get the money from him."

"Sure, Laura."

Her lips opened. She gasped, "Eddie, I'll get it from him. I will."

"Sure, Laura."

She was about to speak again, but now he was on top of her. She grabbed him to her with violence, desperately seeking to merge his body with hers. She began to moan, wordlessly.

Beyond them the light wavered through the trees.

It was just before the final bursting instant that Eddie heard the harsh, drunken laugh. It cut between him and Laura, making his body cold and rigid; Laura's fingers clutched him once more before they fell away from his flesh.

The laugh cut through him again. Eddie swung fiercely to his feet.

"You're a great performer, Eddie," Al said. "A real tiger."

He stood looking up at Eddie and his face was twisted, like it was going to laugh and cry all at the same time. In one of his thick hands was the blue satchel.

The other hand dangled loosely at his side. "Great performer."

Above them the stars hung still in the sky, like hard diamonds. Laura still lay on the sparkling sand, her fingers grabbing at the hem of her dress and holding it down over her knees, her green eyes defiant, yet fearful.

"You look like a virgin," Al said. He suddenly spat down into her face, laughed and turned to Eddie.

"Couldn't you do better?"

"Take it easy, Al," Eddie said. Laura rubbed her face and got up to a sitting position. Her eyes flashed. "You sonofabitch."

Al kicked sand at her, laughed and turned back to Eddie. His gun bulged in his pants pocket. The sky suddenly lit up with a break of heat lightning. Al tapped Eddie on his chest. "What's the matter with Mia? Didn't she give you enough the last time you saw her?"

Eddie felt his muscles tense. "Al."

"One night used to hold you for a week. It doesn't any more, Eddie. You're changing, kid."

He laughed and looked away from them and out over the sheen of the water, out far into the night. His face taut yet sad, the lips thinned into a fine line, he seemed to have forgotten them. Laura got to her feet and slowly moved closer to Eddie.

"You were nothing but a whore," Al said, still looking out at the ocean. "A psycho. And you're going to end up the same way. You'll go whoring in an asylum. I've come to hate your guts. They stink to me."

"You go to hell," Laura said.

He grinned mirthlessly. The dark eyes gleamed. "I'm there already. It's a good feeling to see your best friend on top of your best girl."

"Don't give us that," Laura said bitterly. "All that matters to you is the money in that bag."

It was then, when Al laughed, that Eddie felt his blood run cold. The laugh was toneless, metallic, disjointed.

He's gone over the line, Eddie thought. Then, he added bitterly, we've all gone over the line.

Eddie felt Laura's hand fearfully touch his. Al's eyes glittered. "It's the pretty face that does it, eh Eddie?"

Al's voice fell to a whisper. His hand took the gun out of the pocket. The moonlight ran along its harsh barrel.

Eddie saw Laura go white.

"The pretty face. I used to think it was the greatest, Eddie. They're always the greatest. Like Mia's face to you, the greatest. Mia. That whore, Mia."

"Laura, get the hell out of here," Eddie said.

"Stay," Al laughed. The laughter crackled in the silent air. "Get to the shack."

"It won't help her, you bum. There's no hiding place. Not for her any more, Eddie." He laughed again, his face becoming savage. "A whore's face. You big bum, they're all whore's faces. You big punched-out asshead. Mia. Mia. Mia."

The cruel chant rippled out wildly and threaded through the night. The sweat rolled down his distorted face. He punched Eddie in the chest again and again with the butt of the gun.

"Asshead. Asshead. Sucker asshead. Mia was never with them. What do you think of that? I played you for an asshead. But she's a whore. Like all of them, you asshead."

The laughter became guttural, like the staccato bark of a wild beast. "You were never any good. Just a stumblebum. I led you around like a pig with a ring in its nose. Anything I told you you believed. Asshead. I told you Mia was with them and you took it all in. You got two fists and a big nothing for a brain."

"Al."

"Al. Al. Al. Al killed the cab driver. Al did it. Beat

his brains in and dumped him in the river. He was an ass-head like you. Five bills wasn't enough for him. He wanted more. I gave him more. Over his bastard head. More. More. More. Over his head with a jack handle. He wanted more. The whole world wants more. Whores. All of them. The world is full of whores."

He turned savagely to Laura. "Like this one."

Eddie lunged at him, but Al ducked away and hit Laura hard across the cheekbone with the barrel of the gun. Laura screamed and fell to the sand, her hands clawing at her face. The blood streamed down over her fingers.

"Whore's face!"

"Al!" Eddie shouted.

He lunged again and this time hit him hard on the jaw, with all of his strength. Al staggered back, the gun and bag falling to the beach. His eyes looked dazedly at Eddie. Eddie hit him again, hard in the pit of the stomach, and then a jarring blow to the forehead.

Al grunted and fell to his knees. But the dazed look was no longer in his black eyes. They were now steady and fierce, as if Eddie's blows had suddenly set a fire raging within him.

"I just wanted to break her face, Eddie. You shouldn't have done that."

"It's the end," Eddie shouted. "The bastard end."

"Just to break up the whore's face. Once and forever."

He ducked under Eddie's thrust and butted hard in the groin. Eddie gasped in pain and fell backward onto the sand. Al pounced heavily upon him, his fingers digging for Eddie's eyes. Eddie swung his face away and savagely broke the hold.

They wrestled over the sand and down to the water. Laura was moaning and holding her face.

The bag of money lay up the beach forgotten by all of them. It glimmered on the sand, quiet and alone.

Al struggled free from Eddie's grasp and backed off further into the water, till it came up to his waist. His face was white and wet and bloody. Beyond him loomed the dark stretch of the ocean.

The heat lightning suddenly ripped across the sky, lighting up the two figures with a garish flame. Laura began screaming in pain.

"The end," Eddie suddenly shouted, his voice echoing bitterly over the water. "The end. The end."

And while he was shouting he was hitting at Al, releasing all of his pent-up bitterness and despair. All of his horror and hurt. All of his fury.

"*Edd . . . deeee!*"

The voice came to him as from a great distance.

"*Edd . . . deeee!*"

Then he realized it was coming from the battered face that was Al. He suddenly stopped and looked at it. Al slipped limply into the water.

Eddie stood an instant, dazedly, then bent down and dragged him out of the water onto the beach. He let him slip out of his grasp to the sand. Al lay, face in the sand, gasping for air.

The night was suddenly silent and still. Eddie felt a great weariness spread over him. His knees began to buckle.

"Get away from him, Eddie."

He whirled and stared at Laura. She was leaning against the base of the palm tree, the blood dripping from her face, and in her hand was the gun. At her feet was the satchel.

It was open and some of the money lay spread about her, stained with her blood.

"Laura."

He saw her steady the gun with her hand.

"Laura!"

He started toward her with a rush, but she shot past him, twice. The bullets ripped into Al's body. He gave a great groan and stiffened. His face pushed itself flat into the sand. She fired again and again, the last bullets hitting only the water.

She kept pulling the trigger, even after the gun was empty. When she realized it she looked down at the gun, her face wild and grotesque. Her mass of hair glowed in the moonlight. Her eyes grew very bright, and the following instant the light went dead in them. They stared out to the cold horizon, and closed.

She slid forward.

He got her to the little hospital in Marathon. She opened her eyes once. Seeing the faces about her she weakly motioned them close to her.

"I killed Al Walker," she whispered. "Eddie...is... clear."

Her eyes sought him. Her lips tried to frame his name. But she died.

Al's blow had fractured her skull.

Twenty-two

He stood in the white sunlight, staring ahead of him, a big towering man with a small blue satchel in his hand.

"Doran."

Eddie didn't even turn. "I've been waiting for you," he said.

"I got your message. I'm here."

"Yeah," Eddie breathed out.

He turned and faced the tall slender figure. The Panama hat gleamed in the sun, the brown eyes beneath the brim were sad and grim.

"It's all yours," Eddie said. "It's all there. Not a penny missing. We used our own money. We didn't even dip into this. So it's all there, just as if I never found it."

Ferer took the bag, his fingers closing firmly over its handle. "But you did find it."

Eddie smiled bitterly and said nothing. The Marathon street was bare of figures. It stretched emptily past the motionless buildings and out to the shimmering silence. The fierce eternal sun blazed down on the two men.

"It's over now," Ferer said.

"It's over."

Eddie was about to walk away when the thought came to him. The thought that had been with him a long time.

"Ferer."

"Yes?"

"Who told you about the bank?"

"Walker's woman."

"Laura?"

"She tried to make a deal with me. But by that time it was too late for deals."

"So it was Laura," Eddie said in a toneless voice.

He bit his lip and turned away from the man. Ferer touched him sharply upon the arm. "We get the lives we deserve, Doran. And the deaths."

"She lost all the way. All the way."

"Did you love her?"

"No."

"Mia Alvarez?"

"Let's drop it all. It's over."

Ferer gazed long at the big man. Then he said. "Goodbye, Doran."

"Build me a statue," Eddie said and he walked away from him.

When he got to the little bus station, he went in and stood there before the grimy ticket window.

"Give me a ticket."

"Where to, mister?"

"Anywhere."

"Where's anywhere?"

"Make it New York."

After he paid for his ticket he had only twenty dollars left in his wallet. He went outside and sat down on the empty tree-shaded bench, staring ahead of him. The shadows of the still leaves flecked his broad face. Once he turned and gazed down the long ribbon of the road searching for the bus that was coming from Key West.

He saw nothing but the glare of the empty road and the hard blue of the sky.

There was nobody about him. He sat in a core of silence.

"Eddie."

Her shadow fell across him. "Eddie, please look at me." Her voice was soft and appealing.

Slowly she sat down beside him. And the ache for her began within him. He wanted to tell her of all that had gone wrong with him. How everything he had touched had turned sour. How he had walked a million miles away from the man who went to see Joey Alcan's widow.

A million miles.

"Eddie, you gave the money back," she said.

The sun fell on the oval face. Her dark eyes were large and pleading.

"You've got to forget."

He saw the bus in the distance. He felt her tremble, and her fear went through him.

He kept his eyes pinned upon the approaching bus, watching it get larger. And as he watched, he kept seeing Laura and Al as they were at the end.

"I'll never forget them, Mia. I can't forget them."

But when the bus stopped, he found that he could not get up to board it. He sat there, close to Mia. The driver honked the horn angrily, then drove on.

And when the bus had gone the figures of Al and Laura went with it.

Only that of Mia remained.

THE END